FLYING POETS
& other
# STORYTELLERS

FLYING POETS
& other
STORYTELLERS

On Love Lost, Love Regained, Grief, Regret, Despair and Hope Restored

With Joyful Odes to the Family Cat who made us Laugh Again!

FLYING
with five other creative writers

Copyright © 2024 Flying Poets and Other Storytellers

© Frank L. Ying , Chapter I
© Juliet Smith, Chapter II
© Simon Holder, Chapter III
© Ian C. Stuart, Chapter IV
©Tanya C. Young, Chapter V

The moral right of the authors has been asserted.

Apart from any fair dealing for the purposes of research or private study, or criticism or review, as permitted under the Copyright, Designs and Patents Act 1988, this publication may only be reproduced, stored or transmitted, in any form or by any means, with the prior permission in writing of the publishers, or in the case of reprographic reproduction in accordance with the terms of licences issued by the Copyright Licensing Agency. Enquiries concerning reproduction outside those terms should be sent to the publishers.

This is a work of fiction. Names, characters, businesses, places, events and incidents are either the products of the author's imagination or used in a fictitious manner. Any resemblance to actual persons, living or dead, or actual events is purely coincidental.

Troubador Publishing Ltd
Unit E2 Airfield Business Park
Harrison Road, Market Harborough
Leicestershire LE16 7UL
Tel: 0116 279 2299
Email: books@troubador.co.uk
Web: www.troubador.co.uk

ISBN 978 1836280 361

British Library Cataloguing in Publication Data.
A catalogue record for this book is available from the British Library.

Printed and bound in Great Britain by 4edge Limited
Typeset in 12pt Minion Pro by Troubador Publishing Ltd, Leicester, UK

For incredible sisters everywhere with our enduring gratitude:

Simon Holder for Liz, Ian Stuart for Caroline, Alexia for Saskia, and vice the versa.

And finally, from Frank Ying for Evelyn, May, Sylvia, Barbara, and, also for Edna, whose passion for the written word, art and music kept him and the many siblings sane and grounded to enable us to laugh at ourselves from time to time.

"To all dedicated readers of verse and prose with a splash of art"

Welcome
Bienvenu! Benvenido! Benvenuto!

CONTENTS

I   **F. L. YING**
Osteopath. Gracefully retired. Poet. Author.

Poems from the Heart (1963–2023)   3

Short Stories   113
The Cat And The Bird   113
Cubis Arvina   115
The Ultimate Takeaway   123
Arthouse – An Exhibition Like No Other   127
The Mad Hatter's Tea Rooms   134
Christmas Present   142
A Division Of Spoils   146
The First Lesson   151
The Hitch   157
Mislaid   166
The Introduction   176
The Dragonfly Kite   185
"A Dangerous Riddle Of Chance"   192
The Muse Of Yesteryear   193
Juliet Smith – In Search Of A Muse Once Lost   195

II   **JULIET SMITH**
The muse who vanished off the face of the earth.

Love Poems for an Unknown Stranger (1964–1968)   198

III SIMON HOLDER
Television Director. Scriptwriter. Poet. Author.

Rhymes for Our Times (2017–2023)　　　　　　**220**

IV IAN STUART
Am Dram Actor. Poet. Author.

Poems from the Edge (2015–2022)　　　　　　**240**

Short Stories　　　　　　**259**
The Curious Case of Sandunes　　　　　　259
What, Me Grumpy?　　　　　　261
The Chef's Special　　　　　　263
Four Years On　　　　　　265

V ALEXIA YOUNG AND SASKIA YOUNG
Twin Budding Artists and Writers aged nine.

Alexia Young　　　　　　**268**
Refuge　　　　　　268
Girl　　　　　　269
The Giant　　　　　　270
The Dreamgiver　　　　　　271
Alexia's Diary – Samson　　　　　　272
Fern Electrics　　　　　　273

Saskia Young　　　　　　**274**
Diary – The Shaman　　　　　　274
Mount Olympus　　　　　　276
The Search for Echo's Voice　　　　　　277
Sweet Music　　　　　　279
The Thingy-me-Blob *(by Young/Ying)*　　　　　　280

Flying to Infinity *(by Young-Ying)*   281
A Cat at Sea *(by Young-Ying)*   282
The Life of Gabriela Mistral   284

Index of Images   287
Acknowledgements   289
Epilogue   291

"Literature with its power of words, it is said, is like nectar for the brain and is as honey to soothe the spirit. Like art, it is a window of discovery for truth into our souls. It gives expression to our being – to our very existence and fundamental in learning about all subjects under the sun and not least about ourselves."

Winifred Mary Stuart – Educationist (1905 – 1991)

"The Magical Art of Words"
Alexia Young 2022

CHAPTER I

© **Frank L Ying**

*Osteopath – gracefully retired. Lives in London.
Poet. Author of:*

The Ancestral Quest by F.G.Kwong (aka F.L.Ying)

(Love, grief, and hope through the conflict of war and across the racial divide.
A family's journey of survival from Ancient China to the West)

A Dangerous Riddle of Chance by F.L.Ying

(Murder, mystery, and mayhem in a battle against
the evil Custodians of Terror from an Alterworld

An Anthology Well Lived

Poems from the Heart

YOU BROUGHT…

You brought the spring back into my life,
The buzz, gloss, and sparkle that I had sorely missed.
You showed me blossoms and colours I never saw before,
Of the nature of wonder, birds, and butterflies galore.

You brought the feeling of anticipation of a fresh new day:
The unexpected; the humour,
The hype of a museum or drama of plays.
You showed me how to look at things with a fresh new eye,
To question the outdated, the ordinary,
But never to pass an opportunity by.

You brought a delicate touch into the harshness of life,
To challenge the senses, the scent of the chase.
You kindled the warmth to change a cold night,
The kindness, the gentleness, the subtlety of sight.

You buried the rancour of what was simmering yesterday,
The lull, the apathy that sets with age.
You tested my patience to bait the hook,
The conversation, the smile, the excitement of look.

You gave me the hope that the adventure goes on,
Test the waters, the winding paths,
And the coarse steepness of hills.
You symbolised the promise that days gone are all not lost,
Then to appreciate things we take for granted…
And not a penny of cost.

You gave me a dream, from which we should never awake,
But entwined as individuals, we fought the world as one.
You extended the boundaries that only time can bring,
For your wondrous love-soul which taught my heart to sing.

(C)

SORRY IS SUCH A DIFFICULT WORD

A dash of ink, a hurried thought,
Will that be enough to soothe and court.
Hopefully…

From the tip of my tongue, it's careless talk,
Can that suffice to avert the source.
Angrily…

Dare I utter the things that's barbed,
For is that a grudge you bear so sharp.
Guiltily…

You told me once – a glint of hope is like faith recoil,
It kills off despair to save the spoils.
Tactfully…

You then said – free the reins of being polite,
Protest and run without a fight.
Cowardly…

Yet, another time to save one's face from the start,
If that's easy, speak your mind and honestly impart.
Bitterly…

Trapped under your breath, what did you say?
Pardon. Sorry. I think you must have misheard.
Please, I shan't bite you, why did you stray?

SEASONS OF GROWING

It needs not sunlit shores to think about you,
But burnt sienna grass that I can grasp.
Of all the torrent tempers
That came to cool the summer,
It was the strongest blow
Against the coming autumnal tide:
We once tasted…

Just then,
We felt a shock of dynamite that melted rocks,
And moonlit patches we once shared together.
If I had stayed it would have given me
An anchor for the rest of my life,
Perhaps even then,
I could have believed in a wealth of treasures:
We once saw…

That winter nights remind me of…
Those rattling windows and the violent whistle
From the lonely trains that groaned above the yard.
And the driving rain
That dared to soak the echoing chimneys:
We once heard…

Some say we grew up far too quickly,
Instead of maturing as sturdy bracken all around us
That could have weathered the impending storm.
But then as now,
I could not trade my life for yours again:
We once said…

When thinking back, an old man grows tired
With the guilt of the cross,
He bears with the weariness in days of late.
But aged wisdom creeps in,
To salve and soothe the mind.
And we're much stronger now,
Than as young saplings in the throes:
We once dared hoped…

Now there is no haven to retreat and run to…
You're on your own now,
So, stand tall and face it.
We're braver now than at any other time in life,
For cluttered thoughts are a waste and strife:
We once experienced…

If one could have lived and died in a spell of years,
And lived that magic immersed just for that moment,
It would have served a purpose to tell others
To witness the seasons of growing:
We could not say…

What of the future? What of the past?...
A transient chapter was buried by what's happening now.
It's far richer, far deeper than what went before.
Look back with nostalgia:
Yes. But look forward better with pride.
We can then boast smugly with a youthful smile,
And that will always defy a wizened old heart.

DO NOT GRIEVE FOR ME

Please dear family and cherished friends,
Do not grieve or weep for me,
For I am resting, and I am sleeping.
You have watched over me with much devotion,
Now it comes my turn to watch over you.
Though to you, I may seem faraway,
But do not doubt that I am so nearby.

Dear good friends and loving family,
It makes no difference where you are,
For I will always still be with you,
And looking over you as you look for me.

I question not why this is my journey,
Please accept it so as I have done.
Take comfort in my newfound peace and solace.
The pain has gone, and I am free,
So please let me go but hold me dear.

Just think and speak with joy of me,
But not with sorrow as it will sadden me.
Be brave as I have tried to be…So remember,
That we'll be reunited in kindness and love.

Beloved family and dearest friends,
Do not forget that I have not left you.
I will forever be nearby and always be there,
By constantly watching over you…
And one day you'll stop looking desperately for me,
So go in peace and I will too.

SHOUT PROUDLY HER NAME

Shout proudly her name at every instance,
Her memory will not fade despite the distance.
Talk to her; speak to her your every care,
Though you can't see her, she still will be there.

Admire her courage in her dignified, brave fight,
No one could ask for more, when facing such plight.
Sadly, she was snatched away before her time,
For life seems so unfair when it's so unkind.

But question not why it had to be,
It's in God's plans to set her free.
No pain, no harm can touch her now,
She's resting peacefully glad of thou.

She will not want you to weep for long,
The strength she gave you will make you strong.
Please accept her passing to another land,
To meet her husband again to hold his hand.

Science can ne'er explain the soul that's free,
But have no doubt, it will return in you and thee.
You must go on living a determined love,
Do not fail her, who looks down from above.

Dry up those tears and calm your grief.
You will meet one day, have that belief.
Remember her love within your heart.
As her cherished children will always be a part
Of you, your family and everything you do.
For death is no more when your love is true.

(Eve)

LOVE IS AN ITCH AROUND THE HEART

Spelling the word out, it gives definition for all.
A truth that is pure, though torn full of emotion
In a world full of chaos confused with commotion.
And this I say to you is the core of real love,
It's an itch around the heart that you never can scratch.
It's impossible to say what in the world can it match.

Grinding it down to its basic raw rules,
Love often can dupe us, making us fools.
Though it cannot detract from that ingredient when born,
For love affects us all in its simplest of form.
It began from a child with its mother in view,
Through generations and ages, the bond grew and grew.

Admiring and caring it's much more than that,
Of one's love of nature and the kingdom it holds.
At times seems irrational when feelings grow cold.
There's an unconditional love from its creatures on earth,
For the link between humans is something so rare,
But between you and me, it's the most precious of care.

ABSENCE

I raise no darkened doubts for hope when you are gone,
My thoughts have churned to an abysmal low.
Yet, when you are with me,
I can count the time on the end of my fingers.
Blossoming joy seems to burst out from its seams,
There's no constraint to our words or behaviour in time.
Precious moments to grasp closely – a jewel so refined,
Taste slowly each moment each second of joy.
Chase away those gathering storms that are fear:
Then hang on to hope, to greet and to cheer.

For when you are with me, time disappears in a flash,
Yet when you are absent, it drags so I don't know you.
It's like two separate people, leading two separate lives,
Then it's hard to recall, yet even harder to retrieve.
The face and your image like a ghost to deceive.
Try hard as I might it's difficult to see through,
When depression descends like a veil of red mist.
Banish from your thinking the black clouds of despair,
Meet faith and good hope, it's like a breath of fresh air.

A SOLITARY ROSE

Hers was a single rose with no name chosen to measure,
With a swan neck so graceful reaching the sky,
Its head held aloft seeking clandestine pleasure,
Her heart shivers within it, wanders lonely and by.

The Arctic Rose shoots through the ice and the layers of snow.
The winter wind tries to freeze it, kill it and bends,
Though it stands erect regally and triumphantly shows,
Defeat cast aside, haughtily untouched in the end.

The Rose of the Desert seeks the oasis of light,
Roots dig in the sand as it burrows to drink,
Stubborn but parched, it instinctively fights,
The season's cut short, half an eye in a blink.

But an English Rose of the garden that towers supreme,
Who can pluck that one rosebud to snatch from its crown?
Aloof and angelic, pervading perfume and gleaned,
Impossible to touch as its thorns protect it confounds.

Wait 'til autumn surrounds us with the fall that it needs,
When spring newly arrives, there comes a surprise,
The petals keep falling as its flower goes to seed,
Yet that solitary rose grows again without a disguise.

Even more fragrant and beautiful than the seasons before,
She'll still wait to be plucked and cherished and taken to heart.
Arctic Rose or of the desert can't really compete, even to score,
But their time will end swiftly as her life will then start.

YOU WHO ARE LOST

A dark wind blows that chills the heart,
Damp cobwebs cling, but soon they stutter.
Though cleanse weary thoughts before they start,
Along with some doubts that we dare not utter.

You tempt fate alone it doesn't make sense,
So, harness that hope, regained more ways than one.
All in all, that life renewed will recompense,
You'll soon laugh again. Have faith, *hope* – anon.

IF ONLY HE KNEW

Not so many long years ago when I was at school,
I grew up with a tiny friend called George.
Luckily for us we bonded right from the start,
With his brothers, Arthur, and Henry, both a bit older:
But he was the star of the roost…
For I instinctively knew.

Henry was a weakling and succumbed to disease,
Arthur was brash and adventurous but drowned in a pool.
They were solemnly mourned as we stood by their graves,
Wildflowers we then planted as we bowed our heads low,
And half mumbled our prayers…
In a way as only, we knew.

I asked whosoever up there to protect my pal George,
As he grew up so quickly, fed, watered, and spoilt.
His spindly legs raced around the garden and house,
He grew stronger and fatter surviving each day,
He was cherished and cared for…
As God only knew.

It didn't take long for him to grow up and mature,
He became more independent not needing me so.
For hours he would wander and hide out of view,
Lost from sight it seemed forever but worry I dare not.
Until one day I returned home earlier…
Because I rather hoped that he knew.

I looked high and low for him, getting into a flap,
Corners and cupboards I desperately searched.

Panic stricken I got more anxious as time ticked on by.
'Come and have your supper,' called my father instead.
Sheepishly on his face he wore an odd expression…
Somehow, it was something that only he knew.

'Have you seen my friend?' I hastily implored,
Blank faces surrounded me as the mystery unfolded.
Pointing to the table borne high on a plate
Was my pal rooster plucked, flattened, and baked!
I fled out of the room sickened, then screaming…for
Dreading with horror on the terror he last knew.

JOYFUL EYES AND JOYFUL TEARS

Joyful eyes and joyful tears
When you smiled and ran to greet me.
I laugh aloud to stroke and coddle, elating my ego.
Ah, at last you've disposed of your cold affront,
For you at last are now demonstrative,
Pretending it's spring and the snow had gone.

Joyful eyes and joyful tears,
I grab your chilled hand to hide into my wintry coat.
Had you eventually succumbed to a promise?
To condescend to unclothe that indifference,
An actual slip to condone delight, saying that
You missed my presence after long days in spite?

Joyful eyes, joyful tears, and joyful smile,
Has there been a seismic shift or a drastic change?
Am I ambitious, too presumptuous for those glad deeds?
Apparent to think, oh what deflation; what assumption,
To discover to my shock and horror that
You were merely peeling a pile of old onions!

THE GIRL IN A HAT

He was struck by a girl-beauty in a hat,
She's vying for his attention – whatever is that.
Without wasting time, he then soon fell,
From the very first minute you can tell.
Moving about in a hypnotic daze,
His eyes mesmerised in a hazy glaze.
Talking to her was met with some scorn,
With bored laughter and a scathing big yawn.
His soul's sadness was now torn to shreds,
Leaving a heart yearning that tragically bled.

She's well out of your reach,
As well as your league, many then preached.
So, he put her on a pedestal-kind-of-altar,
Worshipped her from afar and did not falter.
Soon, she changed into a paper-doll picture,
Unreal as a photo with a statue-like stricture.
Until decades passed them by,
When eventually each of them tried.
The hat had long disappeared,
But then fresh love and regret reappeared.
Approaching old age, they both soon went,
Their lives intertwined having just spent.
But then in the end, the story enthralled:
How a simple black hat, started it all.

GAME CHANGER

When I kissed her, she closed her eyes, and I did too,
And the music swelled as a mighty orchestra rose up,
To assault my ears and to rattle my skull.
I look past the pillow to avert her sleep-filled gaze,
My head flushed with joy, as if the brain's drugged in vain.
With a clash of intentions, I grab thoughts from the air,
Silently, I shake because it was no longer the same.
Reality has changed the dynamics of play,
For she became worried, both sensing it so!
But then, I think she began to care for me at last,
And I didn't dare think of it in case I cared as well.
Then all at once, we became somewhat scared,
For both without realising it, a mountain had changed.

THE GAME

When he touched her, she closed her eyes… and
He did too, and the music began to swell in volume.
Louder and yet louder seeming to hurt
When meeting the eardrums that almost burst.

He looked over her shoulder not daring to look,
His head filled to the brim with conflict and joy
For throbbing his brain which fought from the start
As it gasped for clear thought to throw off the heart.

He brushed tears away that fell from her face,
He shivered because, it's no longer a game anymore.
The illusion had changed into something that's real
And then delightfully offended, she began to appeal.

Her guard having dropped just a fractional amount
And he'd dare not think deeply in case he was wrong.
Cautiously she hinted her caring for him at last,
But then became frightened at the thought of the past.

THE GIRL IN A WHEELCHAIR

She grabbed his hand with a wicked smile
When he accused her of being secretly wed,
As he felt slyly being watched by her.
He looked on amused with half-closed eyes,
Cheat and steal by looking demure.

Shaking her head solemnly
When she said such funny things.
He had to grin with gritted teeth,
That her machine had legs that were human,
For she wanted to dance without moving her feet.

Their common wavelength on which they shared,
Became more tuneful when she sang,
At the comic gestures that he then made.
Entertained her to distraction in that careful stage,
Yet he became puzzled at that sullen tirade.

She described she's a river divided the wrong way,
And she's just a fine feather dangled by thread,
But then crumbles away with every gust that impairs.
Whenever, one touches her coursing the wind
But float and float inwards the allure of his care.

Cautiously feeling her way in the world,
Stretching her limbs purposely in an effort to move.
Thwarted, non-fulfilment brought to nought,
The challenge was there waiting, the battle not won,
But he didn't mind waiting; but he minded distraught.
His caring was breezy and light as soft clouds,

Yet never to hurt, to over-suffocate or to possess.
Though her answer to him would still be evasive,
Always unsure by a wavering heart that's confused,
In case his devotion would be much too persuasive.

Poor little Queen Bee, stubborn that's her.
She'll never understand how others genuinely feel,
Many think it's being sorry, feeling sorry inferred.
But perhaps when it happens as the chips are down,
She thought it was just pity; pity the clown.

When days of tired waiting for the months to pass,
In return he'd cry forlorn when she fell ill.
And if she wanted to change things or medication,
Reach out her arms and he would carry her through,
For promises and words only add false expectation.

He removed sharp branches that sprang at her face,
Sheltered her head from the patter of rain.
Cut down the weeds that jumped at her feet,
Covered rough stones that cut in her path.
But it was tragic to think finally in the end,
That his love failed too late for her to complete.

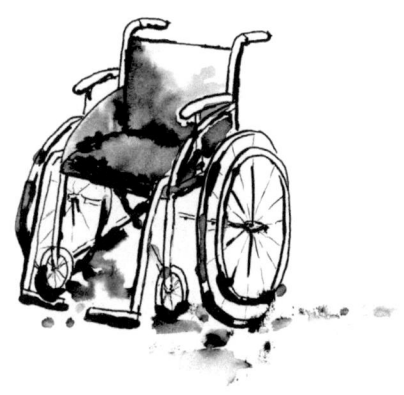

RECOGNITION

If you wanted to smile,
You could create some warmth around the two of us.
And the frosty air glared at you,
Cheated and unwanted.

Suddenly, the vast stretch of water between us subsided,
And I crossed over to you without getting wet.
You suddenly believed that my attention was real:
Really yours without having to give a reason why.

Without artifice and without acting pretence.
We could smile at each other for the very first time,
Honestly and truthfully
There came recognition…

I began to realise that I did not really know you.
Because you offered no stubborn defence
For you bid me glad welcome.
How strange it is to embrace a crystal of discovery:
To discover a friendship -
One of love between two strangers,
Who happened by accident to have only just met?

YOU IGNORE ME

I remember the day before the long wait of yesterday,
You smile and you could capture my selfish thoughts.
Although you pretend with sweet indifference,
You wrinkle your nose up like an angry wild shrew.
And then I noticed for the very first time,
How tiny your ears really were,
'Tis pity you mortgage your heart so deep;
We could resound and sparkle in his absence,
No tell-tale hours or bitter words to keep.

INSOMNIA

I bang my fist like an impatient blow from above,
The reluctant cushion refuses to yield a soft pillow.
Move in restless circles within a rock-filled bed.
I long for oblivion to release the ache,
Of daylight cogs and machined grinding.
My bony knuckles harrow my stone-faced brow,
And even though silken sheets try to soothe me,
Instead become rough seas – violent waves that taunt.
I question why the mind has a mind of its own,
When one tries to aid tired consciousness.

In darkness I see pictures that fade from ordinary sight,
When I snatch vacantly in space at the cool night air,
And I'm still left alone to contend with discontent.
My blankets of shroud can smelt a hot furnace,
Which sweats out the salt from every pore of my body.
The nightmares mock and knock at my cherished hour,
And rides on clouds that used to promise me peace.
Tired hands reach out to curry her favour,
But she whispers cunningly to awake and shake,
And I am left longing to sleep again.

Restlessness abounds churn around my fevered brain.
Some say, it's a honeyed world of another dimension,
For crystallising thoughts and pleasurable pain.
It deceives what it considers the normal behaviour,
Exhaust tired values of a populated day.
Filled with yoked-work and struggle to survive,
Release…yes, release is such tranquil welcome,
When she gives help to remedy the ills.

So, dab off moist fever and try to appease,
My conscience filled with worried consciousness.

Often, I drift and slide into an abstract world,
Of contradictory words and agitated thoughts.
There is no panacea to quell the unwanted,
When suffering hell to fight a new day.
Am I divorced from facing my demons?
A punishment perhaps from another age.
I long for freedom and the spring-like tide,
To sweep away quickly the rush and the cry.
I welcome oblivion and close my tired eyes:
For I'm still longing to sleep again.

A SPIDER'S WEB

I remember your dramatic pauses,
Ruthless arts and fine finished thoughts.
There's nothing meek but for all things might,
Like claps of thunder and ill temperate sorts.
But you are small, delicate, and demure,
So how odd you smile with such strong allure.

Sometimes you act like a spoilt child-diva,
Then create this aura of drooling fawns.
Bait and capture the weaklings around you,
Hoping perhaps, I'd dwindle like your other pawns.
Then, you lash out, protest with different feeling,
Upset all logic, sense, and one's wise reeling.

Is this the way you conduct your life,
To capture all who came to start the race.
Like drunken suitors fall into a trap,
That spiral out of control with a smiling face.
Then you reel me in like a spider's web:
There's no time to resist,
So, willingly relent and surrender instead.

A DAY IN THE COUNTRY

The fresh air from the country longs for peace and seclusion.
But fat women and bony men with their children and friends
Suddenly stream out with willow basket, food, and cushions.
The tired sun desperately tries to hide behind clouds in vain,
Ghostly wisp-like cotton wool, which scud across
The hues of sky-blue, and seem to shame,
The bare-faced face of our tranquil English landscape.
Local inhabitants had seemed to be caught unawares,
After a patch of strengthening sun had suddenly been allowed
To peep through the curtain of cumulus clouds,
As if the tantalising warmth was on ration, merely for today.

But in their wake, the turgid heat scorches swathes of plants,
When suddenly unprepared, their budding leaves so inadequate.
Nature witnesses the dense layers of peopled-hordes arriving,
Who dress down revealingly because of the sudden heat.
Weakened twigs groan, their foliage exposed from heady trees,
Shake helplessly in unison because of the sudden humanity.

Noise and smoke jostle to fight off the challenge,
For space amongst the dedicated joggers amongst them,
Who inwardly aspire to be energetic Olympians.
But the lazy mass of unfit people is in the majority,
That mushrooms and suffocates the keener ones…who,
Rapidly change into assorted shorts and perspiring tee shirts,
Who crowd-out and jolt the rest of the human beings,
By scornfully elbowing them aside into the long dry grass.

Those indolent groups, oh despised human masses,
Pour scorn in ignorance and insult
The soft underbelly of the helpless countryside.
They tramp and spoil the vulnerable grass that refuses
To grow too fast again in our ultra, over-populated climate.
However, save the resilient chains of stubborn daisy
With carpets-yellow of dandelion and buttercups
When horses, cattle and needy lambs need to flee.
But the contented cud of cows ignores the hostile people,
And continues chomping with languid eyes
To enable them to digest and be quite
Ready to process their milk for the morning next.

Across the city parklands and open fields,
Ancient gate post swings open with oil-starved creaks,
And soon collapses by bursting its hinges
To the clambering weight of barbaric children.
Counting the heads as they number in scores to confuse,
The unfortunate farm beasts that carry on nonchalantly,
Who mind their own business and continue grazing.

Suddenly they scatter, and scuttle tail before hind limbs,
As panic explodes as children gleefully unfettered, give chase.
Indigenous flora, sticks and stepping stones across streams,
Abide and shiver, bow their heads down, not to daring protest.
But lo, snip and snap, they fall, and they perish,
And delicate nature crumbles underfoot in deathly silence.
Only for the red-faced girl and bellicose young boy to pull faces
And scream blue murder at the nearest brooding sheep.
Greedily forgetting their need for food and the daily roast
For they receive in return a maternal pat on the head,
With a beam of approval when parents mistakenly indulge.
Freedom unchecked to express whatever they feel,
From their cradle onwards – there's little control.
"But they have been cooped up all winter-

Like caged animals in zoos,"
In mitigation, one could weakly plead for this…
Whereby it's the lamest and foolhardy excuse of them all.

Mama screams out aloud that the picnic's now being served,
The rug on the ground, creaking with fizzy drinks,
And overflowing to the brim with sweet-filled food
From the ice-cooled box which is used just once a year.
Plastic chairs and rickety table now awash with stodgy cakes,
Sandwiches, crisps, and sundry biscuits –
In heap abundance of every sort,
Enough to sink a ship never mind a family or more.

When without warning, suddenly then,
Black claps of thunder rolls over their heads,
Shaking the leaves of the kind sheltering tree.
Raining in buckets it starts to fall
And then the heavens over-ladened, crash right open.
Forked lightning streaked across the sky
And danger and a soaking, imminently nigh.
Hurling up their belongings, they scramble and run
For the dryness and safety
Of their sanctuary in their loyal old car:
Abandoning their feast to the animals
Who hungrily wait, secretly smirking in their fields.

The summer sojourn for the family has abruptly ended:
Suddenly without warning as skies brooded darkly
Like black ink exploding from a giant's quill.
Soaked humanity returned en mass to the city,
Endlessly crawling, dull-grey roads choked in droves.
Relinquishing their claim for now
To the countrified world of the freshest of air:
Although nature sighs deeply, so *gratefully* relieved.

But for now, that cycle will repeat itself again,
The awful dread of waiting…
And trembling for another hot day,
When the heat of the summer dares
Rear its humid head again.
For the life in the country will quake anew in its boots.
And the countryside and green parklands
Long desperately for seclusion and peace once more.

THE RELUCTANT KNIFE

It was a cold dank day in December,
A certain date that he will always remember,
For weeks he had been scheming
Of such an occasion most people would be dreaming,
As he heard rustling in the room next door.

For acting as witness, many others will be coming
To challenge his courage, if not the cunning.
Constantly he's thinking so much was at stake
For there was no room for even a tiny mistake,
When he heard a noise in the room next door.

Deep in his chest his heart thumped like thunder,
Worries rained over him and fractured asunder.
However, many times his plans were rehearsed
It still made his brain hesitate, almost as worse,
As he heard footsteps in the room next door.

Nervously he would huff, dither and blow,
Shaking his head, for it's impossible to know.
There were hundreds of things still preyed on his mind,
Thoughts clashing together, although often unkind,
For he thought of her in the room next door.

Minutes shrank fast, for soon they would arrive
When his time came to do it, had all but contrived.
Regardless, he had to accomplish the task,
His face iced over, like a ghostly mask from the past,
As the handle creaked open in the room next door.

Hot sweat streamed off his face,
The clock on the wall glared at him in haste.
Now his hand was so steady,
The knife sharp and now ready,
When he heard her come into the room.

It was now or never, inevitably it seems,
He must carry on and finish his scheme,
Or face the consequences of failure forever.
Or be laughed at by friends for missing an endeavour,
As she entered the room in a stew.

'Haven't you done it yet,' she shrieked, hands on hips,
Her mouth snarled in mute anger, curling her lips.
Without further ado, he plunged the knife into the breast,
When the turkey half-stuffed rolled onto the floor.
Then she stormed out of the room, slamming the door.

SOMETIMES I WONDER

Sometimes I wonder if I had forgotten her.
My conscience burns of urns of ashes.
Am I living in a wallow of a glorious past?
She would wait a lifetime I know.
But to persuade her,
She'd want me ride, the tiger's back,
And route and rout the world ten times over
To dispel her present wariness.

I loathe her deferent nature; but I am weary.
She must be too, so go to sleep.
I see black mares of hideous dreams,
Of mug-filled air and scalding sands that float
The ebbing tide; the angry rip tide in every season.
They want to haunt and tear at my anguish endlessly.

I cannot help it, but to smell and feel,
The summer day she'd chase the wisp of dusk,
And bade glad welcome to the autumn mist,
Agog the puzzles of adults with a taste of childish joys.
I knew no better; but did I really want to know.

Often, she'd talk carelessly and build illusory castles
With impatient laughter – or was it, real laughter?
At least you smile my fond fooling with no reproach,
Of restless fidget: so, smile and feel,
And so, look again. For I do not mind at all.

I woke up early this morning, long before you ever knew.
The sky was clear and the misted glass from wintry mould;
Seemed so ordinary when stripped of human rancour,

Or when disguised with fictitious gold.
I wear clothes that smell of smoke and stubborn stains.

A selfish moment of wanting myself; my only self.
A feeling of indifference. A feeling of not wanting,
For I do not want her.
There's a glad surge of relief, but I feel sad.
Though I am numbed by the realisation of the addition of time,
When I would never reap that time again: so please grow old.

So go to sleep. Shut off the power of regretful thinking.
Bury wanton thoughts that contempt to please.
Freeze all escape out of our lives for I am seething.
She is not yours now
For she belongs to the dogma of yesterday.
But has she changed? Have I altered with that change?
Though I do not now particularly care.

I create a blanket of dread of acceptance.
Confuse the days and I am lost.
I pretend the stage is mine,
One puppet supplants the other,
Though the image is different, and I become puzzled.
The fading memory raps at my conscience:
Pricking it deeply.
Would she wait and I am left wondering?

WEEP NO MORE FOR ME

Do not weep for me now that you can no longer see me
I will always be there, at the tip of your shoulder
I'll float in the breeze that whispers in the spring
I will waft in the autumn winds that seek you across the moors.

Do not be sad for me now that you no longer hear me
I will never be faraway, just nearby at your shoulder
I'll dance in the sun that gives you warmth in the summer
I will be the nip of the frost that heralds in your winter.

Do not hurt for me now that you can no longer sense me
I will always be there, close by at the end of your shoulder
I'll perfume the scent of the flowers to surround you with ease
I will be the echo of your call in the mountains and seas.

Do not grieve for me now that I am out of sight
I will always be there, nearby at your shoulder
I'll rise in the dawn with the birds on the wing
I will be part of the stars that shine for you at night.

Do not mourn for me anymore because of my passing
For I will always be part of you and your life
As I will always be there at your shoulder besides you
Watching over you with love that is constant and healing.

(Lynne)

THE VAMP

Am I still dreaming as the springs start to creak?
She nudges me hard and caresses my cheek.
Those almond-shaped eyes, those lashes that flutter,
No, I'm still half awake, I dreamily mutter.

Stroke gently her hair, tickle her neck here and then,
Persuading her to desist, once again and again.
I plead, 'Please go back to sleep, it's barely yet dawn!'
'Wake up lazy fool!' she hissed a large yawn.

I smother the sheet way over my face,
'I'm tired, I implore you – you're such a disgrace.'
A rough night has been long it's been a trial of a din,
To snuff out the light that keeps pouring in.

'Get off from my pillow!' I explode and I groan.
For then in return, I receive a terrible moan.
I push her away, but she's now sulking just to please.
She's worse than a mistress to suffer unease.

She drags off the blanket; it's thrown to the floor,
'Please leave me alone!' I hopelessly endure.
I'm shaking like mad, apoplectic with rage…
The fist in my mouth, gagged almost engaged.

Clenched hands circling ready to shove her away.
'It's *not* time to get breakfast,' I hastened to say.
She flies off the bed in a temper disturbed,
I swear it's the last time I would let her demur.

A defiant swish of her body, a vamp in those eyes,
That look of such haughtiness, it's hard to disguise.
She stalks out of the room in a mad fit of pique
For I'll never understand such feline mystique.
Yet again, I'll swear when those nine lives are lost,
I will never replace her, whatever the cost.

(King Lear Poetry Awards 2023. Commendation)

THE PRODIGAL CAT

As the cold winter closed in, he sought out his old home.
He crept through the door flap where upstairs they slept alone.
The night darkness shields him as he lays his weary head,
On the sofa downstairs conveniently made up as a bed.

Like a thief in the night before dawn starts to break,
He flees quietly away hiding no clues in his wake.
Downstairs she trips puzzled, scratching her head,
Each morning surprised something in the night had just fled.
'Why have you ruffled the sofa and my fresh-ironed sheets?'
She scolds her poor husband who shrinks back with cold feet.

One morning as the mist froze ice to the floor,
She awakens to catch a tail fly through the door.
Neighbours had told her of a soul-wrenching tale…
The old cat kept returning, leaving its owner without fail.
Across roads and through fields the cat sought his old house
He missed his old garden, even a squirrel and mouse.

'Have pity on me,' the old cat pleaded without fear.
'This was my home where I grew up over the years.'
She and her husband soft hearted within,
Couldn't turn him away, whatever the whim.
Like a prodigal son returning their hearts were soon won
But their lives were now altered; their routines all undone.

From that day on, he turned them around in his little four paws.
Dotingly they waited on him without showing him the door,
After all this was his home long before they came there,
For he was the now the new owner taking over their wares.
Because the moral of the story, you can now guess the rest,
They became the cat's tenants and were now paying guests.

(Gizmo)

NINE LIVES WELL LIVED

Remember my dearest friends my time has now come.
I grew tired as an old man as the seasons slipped by.
I endured the heat of the summers,
Followed by the frost of the fall,
I have lived a full life in the glow of your love.
This house became a real home when you came along.
Gratefully, I now seek the sun after the long days I have run,
So as, to rest those old legs in a welcoming sleep.

I can honestly confess, that,
My nine lives have been lived to the fullness of life.
Peace, sleep, and contentment, what more can one want?
I have returned to the garden and to the home that I loved.
What's more, I can still be with you looking down from above.
Cheer up my dear friends, be pleased for me now,
For cherished moments of joy,
You have brought to this humblest of cats.

(Mog)

TRIBUTE

Please never forget that I will never forget you.
This love is eternal and etched deeply in the core of our hearts.
No savage illness or earthly passing will tear us apart.

Remind yourself, that I am the lion that roars in the winter cold,
That will seek to shield you
From the Jack of all frosts that try to freeze.
And I will not stop looking over you,
As you have looked lovingly over me.

Please never forget that you are the vital life of my soul,
That captured mine in those sixty-odd summers,
Those long years ago.
And that I will protect you each autumn
Whenever the torrid winds dare blow.

Please remember the time we had just met –
The unique times we had shared together.
A roller coaster of events, a fun musical at times,
We packed life to the full.
How many can say it was a wonderful adventure –
A mix, a gas, a drama, but never dull.

Please never forget that I will be in the drops of rain
As each year approaches. Although
Through seasons anew you cannot see me,
Remember this will ne'er goodbye,
For I will be the colours rich of the rainbow that light up the sky.

I implore you try not to grieve because of what has happened.
Hold onto the fact of our lives were so much loved,
Profoundly enriched and beyond all measure
That brought us lambs delight, newborn in the spring,
And all the sights, so wondrous that fulfilled our treasure.

Please never forget that whenever you feel cold and a little low,
I will be dance in the rays of the sun to warm and cheer you.
For I will remind you of my presence each night
As the air surrounding you turns to drops of dew.

Please remember that you will never be alone,
And so, smile on this journey with me.
I will rustle in the trees and sparkle in the stars
That glow and protect you throughout the night.
Wherever you are, look over your shoulder,
For I'll never be far from your sight.

Please recall the magic we once had …
An orchestral piece that was so refined.
Such soul of my being will never be crushed,
Despite of my body that had finally failed me,
My spirit unbowed, lives on in thee and our beloved three.

And never forget, there'll be no regrets or blame,
For I am resting now and out of pain.
Life described me once, as larger than life,
The lion indomitable that had always roared.
Together my true love, we are, and still forever,
Like an eagle and phoenix, that's soared and just soared…

(Epitaph)

THE RACE, THE CHALLENGE, THE CONQUEST.

Like characters in the fable of the "Tortoise and the Hare".
The story of their lives is a cautionary tale:
It's a salutary lesson for all to share…
His race slowly to the line was nearly done,
Whereas hers like the sleek hare had only just begun.
To take up the challenge of the conquest of her,
His life in the fast lane had become a slow blur.
Was he mistaken by a seductive fleet smile?
Perhaps he was wrong to be so besotted with guile.

Retreat she did behind her cautious brick wall,
Made him more determined to be in her thrall.
Mixed signals from her body sparked confusion to plot,
Convinced him even more that she didn't care a jot.
Drawn into the intrigue of her magnetic allure,
To keep up the chase, he was now not so sure.

To make a move towards her, he did not dare,
Especially more galling if she didn't really care.
Some hint of emotion thought he glinted some passion,
Although it's in her nature to show a bit of compassion.
But he could not tear his eyes from her face,
No clues giveaway about her, but his heart started to race.
With past baggage and traumas their two planets collide,
The wrong timing of each destiny was an inevitable slide.

The careful secrets she guarded were buried forever.
No battering ram or bulldozer would break down
This stubborn barrier of her endeavour.
Although no crumbs of comfort she offered instead,
It occurred to him that he had been mistakenly mislead.
So as, to reach the finishing line of joy…
Did the old tortoise eventually win?
And did the beautiful young hare lose out once again?

TO PUT THE CLOCK BACK
ONE WHOLE YEAR

I put the clock back one whole year and yet,
I am still sipping mists from you.
Wince my eyes tightly; go to sleep,
To want and wind the days back again
To grasp you in my sight.
I fell asleep late last night,
And my head was filled with crystals that rattled.
Suddenly, I believe in a fantasy once more.
Sentiment, "enchanted aroma," to describe,
And recapture a face that came
And went with December.
It's magical anyway.

At least that's what you said,
When you dared to tell me.
Did you know moonbeams and silly things exist?
They came and plucked at my fingers last night.
My eyes were drugged
With hopeless thoughts when you first came,
For I needed sleep so badly.
I remember that cold indifferent winter
That dragged in tandem with the belligerent sun,
And you came with him so gladly.
Scent and magic burst the seams of my eyes,
And I was so reluctant to gaze upon you,
Yet you disconcerted me.

Our silent boldness seemed to precedent all else.
She and he are ousted out without a care.
No guilt, no guffaw to prick our conscience,
No qualms or maltreated sad reflection.
There is no regret…perhaps you felt it too.
I pretend it could never happen:
After all I am older now.

You seemed to reach out with your fingertips
To touch the ends of all cascades
That moved halfway to meet you gladly.
The timber walls of my little room warmed
And glowed whenever you smiled.
Days melt together: one better than before
When especially bathing the sun around you.
Something I cannot help feeling,
That this, the story of my errant life.
But will it happen again?
I really do not know.

I seem to float like a teenage child.
And contentment – being contented filled my mind
With such alarming intensity,
That only hazy clouds and lazy music to think about.
This is ragged and something which half my fault,
And yet half is yours…I blame you too.
At least I argue that I am allowed to.
This happens so many times before:
I pretend that it happens every year…

Is that what you want to believe?
Romantics pledge so at times of full moon:
It is the easy way out.
Take stock of yourself and think about it!
How can it happen to a sanity
And ordinary logic that is mine?
A normal heart is what I harbour and safely guard.
Although you feel my pulse beating loudly
And you chide my brow: however,
I still long to put the clock back one more year.

UNREQUITED

I am wrapped and bound
In a steady force of affectionate duty,
That plays a part in my other life.
But how naive you say!
Yesterday, you told me truths about yourself,
I scoff and scold at the grip of him.
Today I blame you: you blame me
Because both are nicely implicated in the plot.
I look away and stare at the wall,
And I pretend to ignore you.

I resist the temptation of your crystalline eyes,
That dart across the room at my every move.
They sparkle and tremble whenever I touch them.
The very air rushes along the path of yours to mine
Resonates and sings at bursting point.
And yet strangely, nothing escapes from my tongue,
Except baited adoration at such complex beauty:
For I rasp and protest at one's rash duty.

I am embarrassed and blush out aloud.
You stare amiss at the unfriendly floor,
And seems to tilt up your face again
To look directly at mine, just by accident.
Sometimes, I listen for your mood when I am selfish,
To glean and lap up the straw-like hours
That fly by so quickly.

I seemed to have known you a lifetime,
Though what is your name?
I must've met you long before you ever knew.

Did I meet you? Where and how?
This is a dread and awful despair.
What for me is the answer?
What can I say, when you stare so boldly?
My mind and my eyes are susceptible,
To your searching glances that penetrate.
After all, do I disconcert you too?

The cold normality of worldly cares
With its angry climates
That wait outside, wanting to come in.
And he waits with rancorous patience…
Unknowing, dutiful,
And quiet as a partner sleeping.
I tease you with ambiguous phrases:
You flush with anger.
I'd open the door and the cold rushes in
And pales your skin.
I would hide you in my wintry overcoat:
I'm taller than you.

Did you know that I have suddenly grown up
These last few days of meeting you?
My eyes have sunk deeply into my weary head,
That want to sleep but dare not forget you.
I'm drugged with a foul distaste in my mouth,
For my body goes still, rigid, and numb.
My heart, mind and eyes shout out aloud
When still looking at you.
Though poke out my eyes, prick my senses,
But I shall still watch you.
Then there again, it's a love that's unrequited.

TO MAKE ME SMILE

You make me smile when you are a little girl,
Who enthral in childlike joys of fresh green fields,
And country streams.
Nip my hand when I did tease you
Of wondrous fawned creatures and nothing else.
You melt the mist that stains
And clouds the windows,
That shut the dark night out.
I try to grab you in the dimly light,
Save for stubborn fences that fall asunder.

You are a witch. How delightful the change!
I show you off to a darkened mirror which is mine.
You are in plumes of perfumed petals
As I dare to caress the tips of your toes.
I wait and ache in meek adoration
To lightly touch your face – fleetingly.
Although you are rationed ever so sparsely,
And then you shut yourself away
In an ivory tower atop your tall ladder.
I try to reach you and you do battle,
Then retreat to the sanctity of your safe cradle
And try to hide from obvious view.

So, when I call, you would stretch out aloud,
And tumble down for one unguarded moment.
Though I try to catch you when you are falling
For I am the clay beneath your sweetness,
And I would wait a lifetime
To return the charge back to honest niceness,
So as, to give you rosebuds in the dead of night.

Deliver you safe and unspoilt like a golden present:
Exposed into the open for all to see.
But there was so little time to tell you.
So go back to your airy cloud to reassure him:
Or is it you who needs reassurance?

Next time, I shall return in a different mood,
To banish that dismissive look of haughty charms.
You are cloaked in clothes of outward innocence,
Playing a game in an illusory "Role – Fatale,"
For he and me and every mortal to see and witness.
A beauteous picture wrapped in carefree laughter
To capture a photo with infectious joy – then framed.
Perhaps it's a cruel plot to hide true feelings?
So, strip away the mask, and reveal your real self.
And only then, will you make me smile again.

LOVE DESPAIR

I was born a trifle small,
And yesterday of sickly strength.
Movement is pallid, slow, and seized as rust.
The fence you put up is of toughened steel,
Bold, enormous, and despairing.
I caught a side sneak smile of glistening teeth,
And sometimes your eyes seemed filled
With moonstones gleam.
Creep amethyst glass between them.
If I could catch a monster jewel,
I'd insert a precious gem beneath the crack.

You'd make me smile in meek abundance.
Those lithe limbs stretching so lazily.
Could you care if I said yes?
Cross the stream and hold my hand,
Muster steeds and bade me enter.
The enchantment is warm and lucid red.
You seem to sing by mouthing whispers:
It's obvious anyway.

There is a sly shock of knowing when realising,
Perhaps it is real, a hundred times over.
I want to open a door into your very soul,
To seek perhaps a little warmth,
Like a lonely child without a home.
Then a cold rejection, like slamming the door,
Shocked, estranged, but never to let you know.
You wrinkle your nose and shift the movement,
Restlessly, when I look deliberately at you.
Yet no one is watching.
How can they sense,

The sense we feel within our beings.
It's a silent language
That only spiders and honeybees feel,
Though they might be watching…slyly.
You are conscious of this.
I wish I had the strength of patience to wait
And weight you down.
Capture and pluck you out of the air
When you dance before me,
Silently and gracefully like a timid fly.
Please not glare at my face,
It's full of dread and devoid of grace.

Is it too late for us?
Too late to carve a memory, an eternal plot.
Do you know that you belong to yesterday?
Though your glass-like face
Is familiar to me as drops of rain,
And splendid things that adorn
Your petulant voice that tinkles,
Yet you have been spoilt since birth:
Like jade, rose petals and magnolia blossom.
Our special days could never cross.
You belong to a web so deep, involving him…
Long before I ever happened.

Do you know that I am jealous?
I hate this selfish envy though I did not tell you,
After all you revealed nothing to me.
So, it does not matter.
But then again, does it really matter?
You said you were free, and I believed you.
How odd this worship, this adulation of thee
And so, will it end in love despair?

ROGUE THOUGHTS

In the depths of the night,
Rogue thoughts crowd into my head,
Like a fire in my belly
They swirl, and they grow.
A storm in my brain is brewing
And unforgiving like lead.
Problems explode as they tangle
Without logic or flow.
For I helplessly groan …
'Why doesn't the mind lie down to sleep?'
To comply with the night
The sounds silently creep.

I try closing my eyes,
But it does nothing for sight.
Still seeing and hearing –
The limbs wearily toss, and they loll,
For there are masses of ideas competing
And jostling to fight.
To the answers of life's problems
One's determined to solve.

I curse that the mind is a caldron,
An unquenchable thirst.
The turmoil of loud thinking:
With dozens of subjects out of control,
I fear that the burden of sleeping
When fighting the worst.
And the hours drag on slowly
As the body implodes.
It's madness each night,

When it boils to the point,
For the clock fingers crawl slowly
To the hour it appoints.

I scream, *'Keep still!'*
I demand of the runaway train,
The heart is still pounding,
To burst out of its cage.
I sense that the conflicts aren't over yet,
For a tiring soaked brain.
My body is rigid struggling,
The exhaustion outraged.
Then…when dawn breaks eventually,
It's greeted profoundly in relief:
I can fall back asleep soundly,
Restfully, and gratefully deep.

THE GREATEST ITCH OF THEM ALL

'How will I know when the time is right,
To propagate our species?'
Asked he to the giant mammoth,
As he hitched a ride into the Ark
Like a rod on his back.
'The answer will come like a bolt from the sky,'
Trumpeted his host with a swish of his trunk.

'But how will I know if we will be alright…?'
Asked he to the camel passing one another,
Like ships of the desert, well into the night.
'You will know when it happens,
When you live to tell the tale!'
As they scratched at each other bleeding,
And then bristling with fright.

'But how will I know
If we'll survive the flood waters?'
Asked he when he flew to the ass settling in stall.
'There will come a sign from above us,
From the heavens both momentous and tall.'
He replied confidently oozing,
As though he had been through it all before.

'But when will I know when it is safe,
To perpetuate our species?'
Asked he hopped to the ox, nagging him stiff.
'But you'll never know what's around the corner,'
Retorted the anteater, annoyed at the question,
As he sidestepped the animal faeces on the floor.

Then he suddenly swatted
And swallowed the irritable flea whole.
'That'll teach him to ask stupid questions!'
Roared the lion starting to itch.

But the giant buffalo bellowed,
As a mangy mouse scuttled in view,
With another young flea clinging for life in its claws,
It leapt up onto old Noah to hide under his clothes,
Then his beard started to itch horribly
Like unbearable torture. And scratching like fury
Old Noah exasperated did scream,
'Why does the tiniest of earth-species
Cause the greatest itch of them all?'
Though he soon welcomed
The flood waters that suddenly came,
Whilst facing hell in a hand cart
To drown each flea in their thrall.

A WINTER'S SOUL

He stared out of the window willing the frost to thaw.
His heart had been frozen such a long time before:
A hole in his life had been set, carved out to die,
Alone and bereft when left hung out to dry.
The winter snows had blown in early taking him by surprise,
But the impact did little to mend his soul that had survived,
For the seasons had rushed by as she was no longer there:
The days and dark nights dragged long, fuelling utter despair.

Cut off from the world his thoughts lonely and churning,
What chapter happens next, his ambitions now burning.
For numbness and shock had taken its toll,
It had squeezed out his lifeblood draining endlessly a blow.
The warmth from the fire did little to cheer
As lightly it glanced off him, like frigid cold air.
He blew onto the window daring its shadows that cast,
Desperately was he to shake off the thoughts from the past.

Early one morning the icicles slowly melted drip by drip,
The air began defrosting as rising temperatures then gripped.
Out in the garden, he beheld a rose that had survived,
Its petals and colour were strong, whilst still vitally alive,
With its perfume all then effusing, an intoxicating effect.
Enveloped by its sheer beauty he tenderly brought it indoors,
Tended it lovingly, it continued to grow and grow,
His cold heart then defrosted, bringing hope in life's role.
A fresh chapter reborn, for the thaw of the spring
Had healed his tormented soul and transcended all things.

RETURNING HOME

For the greyness and sameness of the buildings
beckoned him home.
Staring at his feet scuffing the worn pavements
he once knew.
He smelled the weariness of the old hedges,
although dirty and sparse.
It still welcomed him back, his heart in a stew.

What had made him leave in the first place
to another town faraway?
He was promised that the grass would be greener,
fresh pastures anew.
As nothing could replace the stark landscape of streets
which were once so familiar to him:
The old corner shop, the grocer, the butcher, the baker,
but to mention a few.

Yet crumbling houses of old neighbours
were long swept away in the slums,
But the church on the corner remained unchanged,
stood indestructible and static throughout all the years.
However, the ancient old local had changed hands,
scores of times trying to keep up.
Although the bustle of ghost voices therein
could be heard still as he fought back the tears.

Choking with memories
he trawled through the town all alone.
That's new, *that* wasn't there when I left,
he thought in despair.
Now overwhelmed with bleak loneliness

he thought coming back was a mistake…
Until he knelt at her gravestone,
feeling he had returned home with her there.

REPROACH

I do not think your attitude requires reproach,
Though your action and words need a little chiding.
However, you could pretend reasonable melancholy.
'It's a throwback from the past,' you plead as a sad reason.
But it's not my fault that I now disown what went before,
It's not my choosing to allow for your mistakes.
It's not my fault that I did leave you.
To pledge devotion is straw and deceptively fake.

Reluctantly to give you a life would betray a promise,
And shackled to the chains of obligation in reproachful love.
We may suffer a lifetime of deep regret,
Within two walls could we ever resolve bitter boundaries,
And melt our hearts as a burning favour.
Then it would thaw the snows that crop on paths
And pull down, stolid shutters that deflect the truth.
But if that happened, then simple logic will be lost in awe.

And harmonious individuals complex as puzzles
Would become orderly and rather mundane.
But to face the future, I prefer the winding road,
That leads to a height that I have never taken.
With no help or support that you will to me
Since you devote your life straight, without a question,
I would fall behind at every step of the way.

We must have the selfish courage to stride out alone.
Dither now, it would be then too late.
So, resolve the conflict and seek to map out your life,
To soothe your needs so that you can make your choice.
Consider it done, then never please hesitate,

You have your spring youth that needs no trumpet season.
For I, my bitter age to think, live in, stare at,
And I to reflect reproachfully with defiant old rage.

DIAMONDS ON FIRE

Her to him, and he to her they locked their gaze,
Staring deep into the pits of her eyes like lovers of old,
To look for the sparkle that was once stored there.
Puzzlement and questioning now filled that space.
'Where did I come from?' they seemed forever to plead.
'But where are *you* going?' he said in reply,
As he drained his glass dry to his empty lips.
'It was a lonely orphanage,' she wailed time and again.
'But I was left on the doorstep without knowing why.'

'Look, you've travelled that journey a million miles over,'
Calmly he rebuked her whilst holding her stare.
But that did little to answer those woes.
Her eyes welled up full of emotion in flood.
Slowly, calm reasoning returned from the tears.
Patiently he waited clenched fists to his jaw,
Then the flame was rekindled like diamonds on fire.
A smile forced a wry laughter that rose from her throat,
For the wine drowned her head, changing her face.

TWO GRACES

Like two little miracles that came down from Heaven
The two of you burst suddenly into our lives.
The sun, the moon, and the stars all at once
As a precious gift you surpassed the want.

Two crystals of magic that grew and grew
Into peals of laughter, gurgles, and smiles sublime.
One fair like the father, the other dark like the mother,
Both beauties defined with wide eyes of the other.

As blazing coals shine in the darkness of night,
Entrancing all who came from afar to see you,
To hold you close, and hug you near
To whisper they loved you without sentiment or fear.

You were intended as a Piscean twosome,
But as Aquarian delights you fitted the bill,
For Mother Nature's plan refused to be heeded,
When joy burst upon us, our hearts-filled need.

People warned that twins would double the work
Yet, at the same time bring double the fun.
They were right, and they were wrong, to employ,
For it quadrupled the work, but with endless the joy.

Grow gently well and healthily oh wondrous children,
Be wise and kind as your beauty blossoms.
Your wholesome nature need not be skewed,
Remember well what life and we have taught you.

Deed not your heads spoilt or be turned around,
But keep those feet firmly well on the ground.
Respect for yourself and those near and adored,
And life will fill with happiness, richness and so much more.

REMEMBER

I remember your probate clauses,
Ruthless arts and fine finished thoughts.
There's nothing meek and all things might,
For thunder strikes and temperate sorts.
But you are small, delicate, and demure,
How odd you smile with a strong allure.

Though, if you wanted to laugh
You would create this aura around you.
Bait and challenge the trifle obvious
And perhaps I'd dwindle like your other pawns.
As a typical child – a bit mundane and often droll
You reach out, propose with diffident feelings,
Upset all logic, sense, and my wise reeling.

How strange it is this simple case of our recalling,
When two strict individuals react with one accord
Who think and feel with a single voice,
And this would scorn our normal thinking,
Replace the humour with evasive choice.
Though, how can you tell when all goes calm?
There is a clue to stop before danger and harm.

Dig into this façade of my indifferent face.
But you tell me nothing as if the past doesn't matter.
I would wish and wait and closely watch you think,
I would scrutinise those with your every word.
Alarmed, deep secrets or real excuses,
And I cannot stop by looking over your shoulder.
But there again you continue to smoulder.

SHYNESS

Keeping her eyes close glued to the ground,
She tried to avoid his disconcerting presence.
In a moment of conscience, he stepped back from the brink,
He was stricken with remorse in case she spurned him.
Because it really hurt harshly, when trying to persuade her,
Preferring to show his devotion than being exposed instead.
It's better to keep a halo around her fair head,
Than a lame lap dog with strong grit in pursuance of her;
As she was the innocent, and he was the guilt
For having disregard for morals or her sensitive feelings.
But then he would never sell his soul in exchange for hers,
When forced to accept the reality: the shyness of old.

TEMPTRESS

Please give a whim of gossamer wings
Which fly beneath the night.
You used to believe in godly witches
That came and marched without much plight.
And jet black hair that never got harried,
A temptress when, having challenged my dreams,
Save once a while, but hath not married.
A speech so grandiose that gestures sadness,
You've thrown down that gauntlet
To reap the danger when milking the madness.

LEAVING THE ANCESTRAL HOME

Weep no more for me your sheltering willows,
For no telltale signs have left of childhood there,
As I had never left home in this friendless place
No footprint stark upon the banks of grass,
No fields of rice to feed me more.
For I have been plucked and cast aside
As corn chaff scattered in the conspiring breeze.
Though now the cold witness of the autumn winds
Would blast a chill through my dead father's soul.
Cry not for me you, restless rivers, and rich bamboo,
For I will return, and return I must, when old,
To be recalled by fresh seasons when born again.

(The Ancestral Quest © F.L. Ying aka F G. Kwong)

REQUIEM

I am the restless wind that blows,
The breeze that lifts you on a summer's day,
To move east and west and back again,
I am the rain that will soothe your brow.
The snow that comes to chill your winter,
I am the ray of sun that brings you comfort,
A star at night, that blinks and fades.
I am the soil beneath your feet,
To weave a path where others might follow.

I am the bough that gives you shelter,
The anchor in earth in the teeth of the storm.
You are the branch that reaches the sky,
Because I am the root from which you will grow.
I am the cord, and you are the thread,
The search for which, that will never cease.
For whom you are, what I am, or for what I was,
Then look no further than to stare in the mirror,
For the river of life will go on and flow.

(The Ancestral Quest © F L Ying aka F.G.Kwong)

CULTURAL REVOLUTION 1966

I have seen through my father's eyes,
Those rampart barrels of gunpowder fire,
Beneath the red flag that flew higher and higher.
And all the sacred makings of a nation once noble,
Swallowed up in days what took centuries to build.
They scattered the ashes of a thousand years.

I have heard through my father's eyes,
A witness seen as he stood alert to see,
That little red book he was forced to read.
Miles across borders he left as a dutiful young man.
Some forty odd years passed before he returned –
Felt mocked as a stranger to trespass the shore.

I remember through my father's eyes,
Startled cries from the people as they ran through fields.
'What took you so long to return to your homeland?'
Alone years ago, I left by reluctant slow seas.
But I now return via the lightning sky.
'Nothing has changed. Everything's the same as it was.'
But through all things transmuted, a mammoth has changed.

I have sensed through my father's eyes,
The path carved out by his fathers before him,
To seek out a new life by crossing oceans and seas,
But the forbears returned bearing gifts from the past.
Forced by starvation and evil despots that war,
Fire, brimstone and burning with upheaval running amok.

I have cried through my father's eyes,
What once stirred a proud nation now destroying itself.
Ancient texts, art, history, even culture, all burnt to the ground.
Clothes individual now banished, with mass uniform enforced.
Poisonous gossip betraying their friends – even a father and son.
It's an edict that's unshakeable that came from the rule.

I have wished through my father's eyes,
That things could have worked out differently, history to change.
Yet death and starved strife were always part of this land.
Separate nations developed through vast mountains and valleys.
Impregnable passes formed barriers to a language unborn.
Scared of all that was foreign became abhorrent to them.

I have hoped through my father's eyes,
The deadly fear in their faces will eventually erase.
The Guards in their madness will come to their senses.
That wilful destruction like a disease would burn itself out.
He had hoped that it would be a passage – fluid in time.
He warned, 'Be patient and be tolerant.'
But for him it was too late.

(The Ancestral Quest © F.L. Ying aka F.G. Kwong)

BALLS OF COTTON WOOL

From a distance beyond the fence and protective high hedgerows,
I noticed miniscule balls of cotton wool-like a-wandering.
Like tiny poms-poms on a bedspread of mammoth green,
Carelessly clinging to the undulating hills of the Yorkshire Dales,
Like soft cumulus clouds in perpetual motion that float.
In innocent motion they gently graze close in random tight circles,
Nonchalantly munching on succulent fresh blades of grass
After a welcome sprinkle of April showers that fell.
Although they daren't wander too far from their matriarchal flocks
Whose cautious eyes keep their charges in check,
In case threatened life by wandering dogs or children on speck.

'Tis ironic to think that these flotsam creatures in gross naivety,
Will soon grow and turn into cumbersome adults,
That lumber about – and I for one, or even young grandchildren,
Will no longer be tempted to ogle with oohs and aahs, or
Drool like fools, seduced by the cuteness of baby-like lambs.
For us being carnivores in our hunger so desperately
Will gladly salivate over them with culinary delight.
Then baste them on Sundays to devour a tasty roast despite!

MOG AND THE FISH TANK

You would grab at my stiff collar between bell and a tag.
I would look down at your shortness beyond a cold shoulder,
Ample coats of long fur to aid you when you're much bolder.
No limit, to discover an unembellished delight,
Perchance that is why you won't put up much of a fight.
I could never stop when staring at you
Like a cat after fish, but never to eat you.
Put you into a glass cage to vaunt to the world,
Such scaled creature-comforts like beauty of line,
Wicked tail and lithe fins, green eyes open that shine.
After the chase, comes the inevitable fall.
Oh, dear you'd be out of my reach as a trophy on walls.

THE DORMOUSE

The cat kept batting this little ball of fluff, as a habit they do,
But it kept scuttling away out of his reach as it flew.
Skidding in panic across the tiled floor
Like rocket of fur, it had crept in from the door,
Effortlessly hiding under the sofa and chair.
The cat in pursuit, relishing the chase and the dare.
'Leave it alone!' I hastened to shout.
It's warm and so tiny, with a tail and a snout.
Cornered and scared it leapt into the bath,
The cat dared not to follow as I screamed in his path.
I rescued the poor creature as it curled up in my palm,
Grateful and relieved that it came to no harm.
However, the chase was too much for its tiny heart,
The dormouse expired giving a sad gasp from the start.

THE OLD OAK TREE

The old lady once stood erect as a sapling's fine youth,
Hunched down on the ground like a wizened old crone.
The world passed her by, her crown collapsed as a hag.
Her arms pared to bone as winds rattled her branches.
'I was young once, as beautiful as thee',
She cried to the skies next to the lithe-like willow.
'Once sinewy and flexible, but strong as an ox,
Even buxom and beguiling to attract people to me.
I have served humanity and nature, dedicating all one's life.
Provided shelter from storms in the height of the winters,
Protected them from rain from the deluge of spring,
And given shade with my boughs from the heat of the sun.'

'Young lovers have carved their names on my trunk,
And my body has borne witness to hundreds of years.'
Yet, then they arrived with chainsaws and even an axe,
To fell this old lady despite of her pain.
Now shorn bare of leaves, her limbs, and her crown,
Her dignity stripped callously as they cut through her roots,
To make way for a road to ease congestion it's said.
Her acorns strewn fallow and new foliage they did shred.
But what did the old lady do to deserve such a death?

STOOD UP

He kept looking at his watch as time ticked by,
Thinking he had got it wrong,
He checked time, time again.
Nervously, shuffling from one foot to the other
The small bunch of bright tulips
Now beginning to fade.
She'd promised to meet him
Under the clock at the station.
'Six o'clock,' she had said sharply.
'Be prompt!' she insisted.
'I'll be wearing a red scarf
Over a dark blue coat that trails.
You can't possibly miss me, my ash blonde hair
Has green highlights to match my long nails!'

Restlessly, he kept staring at all passersby,
Wondering if he'd made a mistake
Of the time – even day.
He mulled over the arrangements
Blindly – making allowances for her.
Having just spoken only once
On the phone at their work.
Trains came and they went,
And yet she still didn't appear.

Time passed by the hour
And he's reluctant to leave.
Thwarted and dispirited
He threw the flowers into a bin.
If only he had waited just a few minutes or so…
For the young blonde searched for him

At the platform opposite next door.
Angry and frustrated
That she had been stood up,
This time, again once more.

WANNABE

At that time, everyone I knew wanted to be someone else
But them, because I was no different when aping a star,
Copying Presley or Sinatra, it was adoration from afar.
The voice croaked along, harmonising with the stereo of sounds,
My talent, so rare I thought wouldn't have any such bounds.
Our friends disagreed and were dismissive at best,
The girls fell about laughing pointing in jest.
'Stick to your poetry, your prose and your art',
Said my teacher of music when he secretly sold my guitar.

Decades came and went, and my wife often teased,
Over my secret ambition when I was nineteen.
But still, I am moaning that I'm a failed wannabe.
Although my life's never empty; as
It's full to the brim with no room for more give.
Now with a sublime daughter as her girls sang in tune,
'Forget it, ole Grampy – *you must let it be, and just live!*'

THE BUTTERLY WHISPERERS

At the bottom of the garden on a hot summer's day,
A little girl was whispering quietly as conspirators would say.
Hidden among the lilac and the dense foliage of trees,
The mother thought it was her sister plotting displease.
Muttering in volumes, their voices carried across,
When their father suspected more like a dastardly plot,

Creeping quietly towards them, parents stole a censorious look,
Preparing to chide them to bring their daughters to book.
Shocked, surprised, and astonished to see butterflies galore,
Red Admirals a-gleaming and Cabbage Whites in their score,
Were surrounding the girls like a storm from the heavens.
When suddenly they noticed the girls
Were, sucking oranges and lemons!

POPPY

It was a hot July day, when I spied a hole in the fence,
Looking around furtively for my mistress I could sense
That she was so occupied with cleaning the flat,
When I noticed the path, which was well worn by cats.
Sniffing my nose through the flowers and the weeds
I saw two young girls beckoning me to come play. *Please!*

Scrabbling so low through the gap so well tread
The girls whispered encouragement, please hurry instead.
Nervously approaching, I looked at them near
They stroked and they tickled my fur without fear.
'What are you called?' asked the fair blue-eyes,
'Don't be so silly!' said the dark-haired in reply.
'She's only a pup who can't talk from the flats from behind.
It's an old people's home!' she said, trying to be kind.

It's an exciting new world out here, I wanted to stay,
The girls have a big garden with trees and a balcony bay.
Fussed over and over they fed me biscuits galore,
They brought out a ball and I chased them yet more.
Then, suddenly from behind, I heard a terrible shriek,
'Pop…*POPPY!* Where have you gone?
I was so scared to speak.
'I've made new young friends, who are agile and fun!
I knew in my heart, I might be punished, really undone.'

Fair blue-eyes, crept cautiously up to the hole in the fence,
'Heh. Mrs, the doggy is here!' shouted she in defence.
'She's safe and she's happy,'
Added the dark-haired one, holding my tail
But the high-pitched demand from the fraught owner did wail.

'Oh children, push Poppy through, so I can grab at her head.'
But the dog, stubborn creature, dug her paws in instead.

A large pair of hands poked through that small gap,
Grabbed at her collar, yanked blindly she hollered,
'Next time you run away, back to that dogs' home you'll go!'
Poppy returned to her mistress, sheepishly safe, but aglow.
Sad and forlorn the girls trooped back to their home,
When they screamed out loudly in vain to their mother,
'We WANT a real puppy, a soft kitten,
Or something FLUFFY, furry, or other!'

TO EMBRACE THE SEASONS

As the dark nights of winter draw in, closing its drapes,
We'll miss the sun's tonic and the bright light of the morn.
But I implore you to look out of the window nearby
For what can beat the panorama of nature renewed?

The drops shimmering of dew on the leaves from last night,
Remain in clear clusters from the sharp heat of the day.
The golden leaves of the autumn cascade down like confetti
To carpet the streets as the trees shake their crowns.
Facing the wind and the mist, it whips up from the ground.

I look forward to the vista of pure magic I see,
The fat-bellied smug robin, his scarlet breast all aglow,
Balanced snugly aloft on prickles, sharp-green of the holly.
I smell the crisp snows, white-pure of the winter
With abundant ripe berries amongst the scattering of thorns,
Dense blood-red as a blanket choking the view.

It's going to be a harsh winter, forecasters do say,
And so, get ready, embrace it, so take a deep breath.
The hoar frost etches art on the panes of the windows
And snow that's so thick weighs down on each bough,
That kisses the ground, blending a landscape unique,
A picture so perfect, it knows no infinite bounds.

Fear not that the cold season will last forever anon,
Inevitably spring will follow on the coat tails of winter,
As moonless nights follow the dull of the day. Meanwhile,
Absorb sight of the snowdrops, irrepressible as new life
Thrusting bare heads through the frost and the snows.
Then suddenly, crocuses stall, as primroses abound
To dominate the hedgerows in chrome-yellows of spring.

Although another year passes with its ending that soon dies.
Perhaps regretful of the time that we'll never taste again
For days hurtle to the end station like a train fast on the rails.
But look around you to taste nature wondrous once more,
Its beauty surpasses all things one imagined in fantasy minds,
Sustaining our souls and feed spirits that have lagged.
Thus, cherish it as a fresh fountain to rejuvenate our past.

And so, let's live life again to fresh pastures anew.
Embrace each new season to welcome its reborn,
Let imagination run riot to unshackle optimism with hope.
Search beyond your horizons and marvel with infinity of joy.
Then humanity can look to the future to continue that spirit,
To reach forwards always – but never backwards again.

THE KEEP FIT FIEND

Each day he would spend his spare hours at the club gym,
He was dedicated as mustard, to make himself trim.
Carefully watching his muscles with Latin names as such,
Gluteus, Quadriceps, Triceps, and others just as much,
His biceps enlarging and the Lats and the Core,
His wife was concerned, her growing anxiety ignored.
Proud six pack on his body developing anew,
He would sweat and he'd puff, getting into a stew.
Expanding to bursting point, using all weights galore
Dissatisfied with his efforts, he wanted much more.
Bench presses and dumbbells increasing in weight,
But his erratic cardio output will decide his fanatical fate.

Diet and avid exercise consumed most of his days,
It left no time for his work or the necessity of play.
The treadmill, the cycling, and the protein-pure shakes,
Hours married to the machines became his mistake,
Only added to this mania for bulking his frame,
Hope for the title *"Invincible"* to add to his name.
But one day, this obsession took a dangerous turn,
He went far too far, as he went for the burn.
Muscle-bound and locked-in he could barely but walk,
Osteopaths and Medics had failed in their warning talk.
'You'll exercise excessively for one's norm to behave'.
But the keep fit fiend ignored them and went to his grave.

FAITH, HOPE AND JOY REGAINED

This is not the end of all things,
But really the beginning…for
Fresh seasons are turning a new page in its life.
The scorched earth has fought back
From the sickness and ills.
Like wide-eyed young children
There came new evergreen shoots.
It is growing again
Despite the recent fire devastating the world,
As with rays of pure light glistening
Through the dense wood and the trees.
You can see the branches renewed,
And the rich carpet of leaves
With the uplifting sight of a child-innocent
Skipping in joyful abandon,
In faith, hope and much laughter,
Irrepressibly reborn.

ANIMAL GRACE

Lord, save us from these restless waves,
And violent storms, you try to save.
These Lands so fair beyond our gaze,
With all man and creature caught in a daze.
We swim in waves of human face,
Pretend a life of animal grace.
And reflect our deeds, the way we treat,
All God's good creatures we think as meat!

(A Dangerous Riddle of Chance © F L Ying)

A CAUTIONARY TALE FOR JOYRIDERS

Whistle while you work,
Some people are such berks!
They leave their cars with doors ajar,
No wonder gave us perks.
Some have been misled,
Soon they'll lose their heads.
Their cars have gone instead.
Whistle while you work!

(A Dangerous Riddle of Chance © F L Ying)

FOR CREATURES' FIGHTING ARTS

Outwit by brain or defeat by brawn,
Whilst thou win or err be torn?
So, remember; speed and guile will make thee smile.
Brute strength and curse will make things worse:
A jumping beast will teach thee first,
His flexible frame has one big purse!
The stance of a wild horse will blow them off course.
Wings of a bat are powerful as the might of a wild tomcat.
The tail of a dragon can sweep away wagons.
Yet the claws of a lion are stronger than iron.
A beak of a crow will bend even the strong bow.
But the vision of man will defeat all he can,
By guile of his cunning, his enemies will go running!

(A Dangerous Riddle of Chance © F L Ying)

WAITING FOR HIM

For thousands of years,
We've waited in wait to decide our fate.
For a humble-fun one, not man, nor ape.
Will evolve from a tree, no cynical ploy,
Bringing happiness and peace with unconditional joy.
No man, fish, fowl or beast will eat each other in feast.
Though Mother Earth so precious, given on loan.
Serenity at last, no longer will groan.
Thrust into our mist, oh timbered fat clown,
We appeal to your power – help if you can!

(A Dangerous Riddle of Chance © F L Ying)

THE FORTUNE TELLER

Oceans of treasure, so vast and so old,
Temptation is hard to steal all of its gold.
Whatever the fortune, it's all in the past.
Whatever's the future, it just cannot last.

(A Trilogy of Chance © F L Ying)

THE CURSE

Oh, mocking curse, mocking curse, try not to catch me.
Too late, you're so stupid attempting to flee.
Per chance you're so clever, always you think,
So desperate, not falter – return from the brink.

With oceans of treasure, so vast and so old,
Temptation tries hard to float all, of its gold.
But by chance you control the earth and the seas,
There are dangers that court you with fatal disease.

Though forbidden to danger, the Tree of All Life:
All you will find is curse…death and strife.
Kill all your good laughter; it'll make your spine curl.
A watery grave awaits you to part from this world.

Dare chase all life's dreams – a trail out of bounds.
Like fools follow the end, its death down to clowns!
Poke out all their lights that came quite by chance,
Wipe out all the joy without conscience glance.

Oh, mocking fool, mocking fool, why try to catch me,
You're too late – you're too feeble – desperate to flee.

(A Dangerous Riddle of Chance © F L Ying)

THE TREE OF LIFE

It was from a tiny seed from within a small pod
That is where nature began its secret of life.
It grew without prompting requiring just enough water
To nourish it as it searches for the beacon of light.
Its roots clung to the earth as a foundation of youth,
Fertility-bearing one day the fruit as it grows.
With bacteria and microbes, it lives in symbiosis,
Entwined within roots fed by the nitrogenous soil.
Dioxide of carbon it absorbs as the lungs of the earth,
Releasing oxygen in turn for our lives to sustain.
Rain falls down to earth to be recycled again.

Photosynthesis as the prime genesis, bound up in its leaves.
How did these nutrients weave their way into sapling, then tree?
It's explained by the science of osmosis to laymen like me,
When aided by matter excreted by animal and our bodies decay.
Both human and creature go from ashes to mere dust
To provide these new ingredients as food for the store.
Then repair and renewal, every hour, day, and night,
The structure grows stronger in size and in might.

Bursting with berries proudly, as its offspring it shines,
But the birds of the feather pick it for food on the hoof
For not only unexpectedly we feared that they could.
Then man feasts on these creatures as naturally he would.
This chain of events continues the vital life cycle,
From cradle to grave, an embryo starts life in all and in thee.
For one day before long, the proud foliage reaches the sky:
Such wonders of science like this phenomenon *will* not cease.
But the world questions God's creation in order to thrive,
When giving birth to earth's miracles like this tree of all life.

WHAT IF

What if…
He had shown that,
Only you would see if he laughed or smiled?
If only one knew how a fool must feel.
What if…
He had revealed those,
Tears silently stream; concealed so deeply.
Could it touch your heart that's genuinely felt?
What if…
He had pledged a
Glimmer of hope which was a deceptive token?
Applause from thee are words unspoken.
What if…
He had tried, but
You turn a cheek and love that's just been.
But can you still mend a dream that's broken?
What if…

(A Trilogy of Chance © F L Ying)

WHAT AM I DOING HERE?

What am I doing here?
She doesn't remember our days of glory,
The children of light:
The sunlight hours
And its amber setting we once shared.
Those open skies of optimism
That once beckoned in front of us.
Does she still remember,
Even a hint of whom we once were?

To recall the fresh excitement
Of our first meeting.
The walks in the spring
And the summer hills of kindness of love.
The journey of hearts discovered,
Never travelled before.
She looks blank at the wall,
And doesn't recall the fountain of youth.

What am I doing here?
She stares at my face,
As a stranger or carer
Looking through right through me
As if I'm a glass window,
Transparent and brittle,
Not even a ghost from the past.
Her face is placid, hardly engaging,
Now bereft of all feelings,

Because there's nothing
To get anxious or angry about.
The conversation is now just one way,
That ebbs and flows.
It's an effort supreme my trying to cajole,
Even just a tiny response,
To dig and to remind her
Of our years shared together.

What am I doing here?
Are memories of yesteryear-battles,
And triumphs, buried forever?
But I fear they are gone in the ether,
Wiped clean like a slate.
Have they evaporated,
Like dust motes in the air around her?

The touch of my hand changes little
And reminds her of nothing.
An embrace is futile, because…
She recoils from me; but I'm not shocked.
I drone on about matters mundane,
Because the past doesn't mean a thing.
She doesn't remember me.
But then I, remember her.
And that's why I am here.

A NEW BEGINNING

This is not the end of the beginning.
Neither is it the beginning of the dread-filled end.
It is in fact the start of something anew.
Because out of gloom comes a new dawn,
Fresh hope and a new joy having just been reborn.
The suffering has now finished,
A new page of life has been turned.
After the storm, a rainbow glows bright.
Darkness has been replaced
With the optimism of light.

A SIBLING THREAD

I realise now,
There once is a bloodline thread
That was a bond that was unbreakable
Between a father and son.
From the beginning of life,
It increased as years passed us by.
Like an umbilical cord tightening
Close from the start,
Its blood binds indivisibly as one unit.

A primeval urge from a child to an adult
An indivisible love thickens and grows.
But on the flip side of the coin,
A distinct rivalry ensues.
Paradoxically, the father attempts
To influence his son,
By installing a mirror image of himself,
As a fixation from his youth.

Although it is no different
In the animal kingdom,
When males in the pecking order
Fought to be dominant.
Is this rivalry and snare the same,
Between siblings in all creatures?
A fierce competitive streak
From the gene pool from day one,

From primordial times
When humans first strived on the earth.
Then is it a protective mechanism

In the face of all threats
For survival of the family,
Regardless of the species?
But then I must try to reconcile it now
When facing the cliff edge of life.

Meanwhile, from father to daughter
The closeness has been unshakeable,
Unchanged from the outset; set in stone.
Because this time there happens
To be an empirical difference,
For it's not one of *competing*
But bound close from the cradle.
Perhaps it's identical to the thread
Between a mother and son –
That the unconditional love cycle
Starts all over again.

LATE

Am I late?
So many important things
Have been unsaid
That should have passed between us.
Then time tragically suddenly flew past
Before we knew it.
Where did the days?
The years, crucially retreat.
Was it hidden behind
A curtain of shame?
Or was it stuck in
One's foolish false pride?

Am I late?
What on earth did we quarrel,
Really about?
Observers will say it was trivial at most.
Yet when all one's trite actions
When rebuked, spat unchecked,
And criss-crossed the room.
Misconstrued and cruelly screamed out,
Thereby designed stupidly to wound.

Am I late?
Did we have much more in common,
Rather than fundamental differences
That bound us once,
Like glue as peas in a family pod?
Remember there was once from day one,
An extremely strong sibling love…
A bond so strong and impervious

That it was almost unbreakable:
That some will say we were almost joined
At the veritable hip.
Which was more important than
The petty trivia that came and divided us.

Am I late?
Perchance we had changed drastically
Into foolish rivals to compete,
That had contributed to our dire despair?
But was it nigh now impossible
To repair the drift.
In this earthly life, am I now
Too old to make amends?
For this remorse of mine so deep
Came too late of sorrow:
Became overflowing to the brim
And filled with the deepest of regrets.

Am I late?
I wanted to say that I'm sorry I did hurt you.
I realise now that all such words,
Whether innocuous or thought then, harmless,
All bear consequences.
We needed to heal fences
With the sincerest of moves,
Rather than pretend symbolic gestures
Using the feeblest of excuses.

Am I too late?
As time is now against us,
And especially at this moment.
For it happened sadly,
Suddenly without my even knowing.
Because ultimately one day,

I will face mine own maker,
Who will judge me then,
When protesting my futile, weak excuses,
Then desperately hoping for a reconciliation.
Although I must confess
From a redeeming aging heart,
That I'm *really*, sorry,
That I had arrived now far too late.

INSECT AND MAN – HAMMERING AT THE GATES

If I for one, an indulgent winged species
Could write a thousand words,
They would not suffice
To mimic noble thoughts of man
When hammering impatiently
On the Gates of Paradise.
Given the fervent wish
Of all mortal creatures that seek redemption,
This I bear witness vividly then –
By staring enviously.

I see a melancholy one
That stood back waiting in his place,
Although unshaken on the hostile path
He waits impatiently…orderly,
Next to be saved.
Then watching with nervous trembles
Until his turn came,
Shameless and arrogant, his head unbowed,
But proud as a peacock's crown to face,
On side lines concealed
Close to bare human flesh.

I hear aloud as much
As brass trumpets blared
Bellicose, belligerent
As his last breath expired.
Achieved not what was gained
On one's selfish earth,
Boast rage and temper
That roared unchecked.

To hang on to life
By strong fingertips clawed,
And scream and cry,
To curse and shout.
Though on instinctive whim
I follow him unquestioningly,
To take my turn to enter
Via those precious portals.

But simple man felt betrayed
When seeking his last vestige of air.
That was snatched away
From him before his time.
He confessed that he,
A person flawed like shattered glass,
Although can one still be allowed
Through the sacred gates despite
Those earthly sins, they flouted,
In flagrant breach of worthy deeds.

But I'm about to protest it is my turn,
Oh, delicate one.
Then all perchance abruptly squashed
Flat against paled cheek,
As a palm of a hand slapped me dead,
As do irascible insect's fate.
Only then, too late
Did it suddenly occur to me,
That this hallowed sanctuary
Was only meant for human life,
For man and woman and they, alone.

BLUEBELL WOODS

Please do not cry for me now that I am gone,
I will still be there in the scent of the morning dew.
Search for me in the comforting warmth of the midday sun
That scatter through the branches of the sheltering trees.

Please do not despair for me now that I am resting.
My journey from life to ease my weary limbs has just begun.
But you will still see me dance in the light of the stars
That sparkle for you in the beams of the moon each night.

Please do not grieve for me now that I am no longer with you,
For I am now sleeping and out of pain.
Remember me throughout all the seasons – because,
I will always be there, watching over you wherever you are.

Please do not fret for me because of my passing,
Come rain or frost, I will always be here,
Still caring over you with a love that's constant.
So, look out for me amongst the fresh bed of bluebells,
Which will renew and come alive in me, every year in spring.

THE CAT AND THE BIRD

The cat stared intently at the large bird holding his gaze. 'You know, you birds seem to know such a lot more than most other creatures around us. How do you do it?'

The bird cocked his head to one side thinking seriously for one moment. 'It's because we fly all over the world picking up information and wisdom on how it all works. You must have heard for example, that our cousins the swallows migrate each year halfway around the globe to South Africa and back without drawing breath. *We are the only species on the planet that can fly vast distances.* We follow magnetic earth lines. We are guided by the moon and the changing movements of tides. We eat, sing, sleep and can even visit the loo in mid-air…And sometimes, all at the same time!'

He pushed out his chest with unadulterated pride, smoothing his ruffled feathers. Without prompting, he broke into song, hopping up and down, as well as sideways on the kitchen table with an arrogant glee.

> 'Ah ha ha. It's great to be a bird.
> Special species we're always heard.
> As copycats (looking at the cat sternly in the eye)
> And other creatures attempt to fly – the fools.
> Ha ha. Tee hee, they fall to sea then die.
> Aha. Yes siree, it's brill to have the wing.
> Oh yes, ha ha, only we, a voice unique to sing.
> It's great to be a bird.
> It's really grr-eat to be a bird.'

The cat was so taken aback that he didn't applaud. There came a palpable silence that you could have heard a feather float to the ground.

The embarrassing lull was suddenly broken by a gruff voice in the back of the kitchen sneering.

'Pigs 'ave troiyed. So 'ave 'umans. Ands a blinkin' right 'ole mess they alls mades of it. Just looks at thats foreign fella of yonks past, ole Licorice Sticks, oose waxen wings melted in them rays of the sun… the loony lunatics', shouted the farmer sarcastically.

'Don't you mean Icarus?' offered his wife nervously in the face of her husband's scowl.

Then in one abrupt movement, the bellicose figure of the farmer pushed back his chair with a sudden squeal, scraping the floor and started to stomp out of the room in a rage. Cocking an ancient old shotgun in readiness, he spat out the clod of tobacco that he was chewing and started to mock from the back of his throat as he prowled around ominously.

'Birds of a feather stick stupidly together.
Those of a kind are just as blind.
Birds like fowl are foul with words.
And crows or parrots talking are just absurd.
Their wings to be clipped – being only fit to be shot,
Then de-feathered and boiled for supper in pots!'

(A Trilogy of Chance © F L Ying)

CUBIS ARVINA

It was the year of 1453 – during spring, to be exact, in the tiny principality of Hysterovia, when its all-powerful monarch, King Rupert the Bold declared a day of radical cleaning and all-encompassing, scrubbing throughout the castle environs and the whole kingdom. Spring cleaning of the castle and the surrounding hamlets was decreed as a national event imposed on all its citizens of Hysterovia after years of wallowing in a miasma of thick dust, filthy cobwebs, decaying straw, and animal manure leading to deadly plagues and virulent pox that had besieged their living quarters. And this was not to even mention decades of neglect of personal bodily hygiene or that their owner's foul-smelling undergarments had not been washed or had not seen the light of day for years. Noblemen, soldiers, traders, farmers, peasants, and servants alike were expected to obey the royal decree of cleanliness on the fear of punishment most savage from the Crown.

And so, on that auspicious day – the first of April to be precise, King Rupert left the castle with his royal entourage to visit his cousin, one hundred miles away in the neighbouring kingdom of Pandovia. He left strict instructions for his forever indolent son Prince Claude the Languid to exert himself manually for once in his cosseted life, instead of spending his hours eating, drinking and womanising which hitherto consisted of a continuous round of indulging his voracious appetite with endless flagons of aromatic meads, fulsome ales and exotic wines, as well as roasted virgin swans and enormous charcoaled-fired steaks of tenderised venison from the royal estate and the surrounding forests.

His dedication to the ways of the flesh was much to the despair of Agnes the loyal cook, who had noticed that the prince's already ample girth was getting wider and wider than even that of her own. But very much heavier – so much so, that having grown so obese that he broke several beds in the process. Typically, he would gorge to the full, belch loudly and vomit the half-digested food into a chamber pot. Then he would start all over again.

'I command that you rigorously apply yourself physically and usefully my son to set a good example to the court, the servants and the people of the realm!' ordered the monarch as he set off on his journey.

But, as soon as the royal carriage was a distant dot on the horizon, observed with considerable impatience from his vantage point on the front battlements, Prince Claude, without wasting a single minute, hastened into the dining room to demand more platters of succulent, freshly cooked food from the kitchen to appease his greed – only to be met by Agnes the cook blocking the door.

'Your father, the king has instructed me and the kitchen staff not to indulge you, until you show signs that you are willing to carry out his wishes and do some hard physical work by spring cleaning!'

Hands on her ample hips, Agnes stood her ground and was adamant this time not to weaken in her resolve, and give in.

'I have been instructed that you are to apply an unlimited amount, of *Cubis Arvina*, that is, elbow grease to polish the throne rigorously, and to spit and burnish all the walnut furniture in your chamber until they shine like a mirror. Until that time, I have been ordered only to serve you water from the well!'

The prince, extremely fearful of his father's wrath, and daring not to cross Agnes in case of not being fed his favourite foods, thought that he had better comply, whilst at the same time complaining that menial tasks such as cleaning were meant for servants and for those of commoner class and not for persons such as he of royal birth.

But, as it was his wont when he did not get his way, he chose to bully his servants and throw his not-inconsiderable weight around, thoroughly convinced that everyone he encountered were his inferiors. And bully mercilessly he did. His favourite whipping boy – actually, a whipping girl, was the palace scullery maid who was also underling to the chamber, one Clastara. Fair-haired, skinny, and timid as a church mouse at five foot nothing in her bare feet, poor shy little Clastara was the subject of the prince's constant baiting, taunting and trickery after she had rejected his drunken advances in the wine cellar last summer.

Calling his footman, Prince Claude bellowed, 'Tell Clastara, that insolent girl that I have an important errand for her!'

Clastara hurried from the scullery as soon as she was summoned to the antechamber. She nervously curtsied to the prince, not daring to look him in the eye. She stuttered with trepidation.

Towering over her, Prince Claude thrust a note into her shaking hands.

'I want you to go immediately into the village to seek out old Sagacious at the apothecary for him to dispense what I have commanded for in this letter. It is an urgent request for a handsome pot of Cubis Arvina, formulated from nothing but pure royal ingredients that will enable me to carry out the King's instructions. Once that is in my hands, I can demonstrate to you, and the surly likes of you, and all similar slothful, useless people here – of what *real,* hard manual work feels like in the kingdom!'

No sooner had he uttered these words, he gave a half wink to his footman completely sure of himself that this situation was *never* going to happen.

'Now if you return with my instructions *fully* complied with, then I shall go about to set a royal and fine example to the citizens of Hysterovia by earnestly applying myself to clean and polish the castle rooms from top to bottom! Concurrently, I shall also unselfishly forsake my favourite sustenance of barbecued wild boar and spit-roasted, stuffed peacocks in lieu of the task ahead,' he added with some reluctance.

'However, if you *fail* in this simple task, you, miserable girl, you will be punished thirty-three times. You will be strapped in the ducking stool under the drawbridge when the moat is full of murky water after the emptying of the chamber pots at noon, and then thrown into the dungeons for good measure! Now begone with you! Hurry, you wretched wench. Now and get out of my sight!'

Clastara gave a half-curtsy and backed obsequiously out of the room, trembling like a jelly.

In much haste she descended the backstairs into the kitchen to get her shawl for the journey. As Agnes the cook passed her on the stairs, Clastara mumbled miserably to her about the royal command for a pot of the special grease.

Suspecting some treacherous plot in the offing, Agnes tried to call out. 'Heh! Just wait, young Clastara. I must warn you that there's *no such thing as…*'

But by that time, Clastara was out of earshot and halfway across the courtyard heading for the castle gates.

Reaching the old shop of the village apothecary, breathlessly young Clastara pushed open the door, tripping the little brass bell on the door frame to announce her presence. From the back of the shop through a beaded curtain, old Sagacious, his spine crooked and arthritic over years of bending over endless specimens and scribbling out complex formulae through a magnifying glass, greeted her in a hoarse voice that emerged from the back of his throat like a trapped frog.

'Good day to you young Missie! What can I do for you?'

On being handed the royal warrant with the official seal of Prince Claude, the old man perched his half-moon glasses on his nose and hurrumped and groaned with a deep sigh. Then on breaking the seal, his eyes grew bigger than over-ripe pumpkins. There was an audible hesitation.

'But, but…Missie, there's no such thing in the whole of the land such as *elb-ow gr…*'

His protest trailed away as he swallowed hard. Then seeing the forlorn look of terror on the young girl's face, he realised immediately the terrible punishment that was waiting for her, if she did *not* return with the prince's instructions specifically fulfilled, not only in its entirety, but *exactly* as the prince had ordered. A dreadful dilemma enveloped him.

'Sir! My good sir…' she mumbled staring at her feet, as a tear welled up. 'I *have* to return to the castle with what my master's wishes, *exactly* as instructed in his letter!'

Overcome with anxiety, Clastara then told the old man of the terrifying fate that awaited her if she failed in this endeavour.

Shaking his head like an old sheep dog, the old apothecarian scratched his chin thinking, when he suddenly thought of a brainwave had just been lit between his ears.

'Um. Just wait here young Missie. I'll see what magic I can conjure up. I have an idea. But I need to summon my ancient texts from the old manuscripts from hundreds of years ago from the ancient formulary of Materia Medica!'

Abruptly, he then turned on his heels and went to the back dispensary through the beaded curtain which parted involuntarily as for Moses in the Sea of Galilee.

As Clastara shuffled restlessly from foot to foot to kill time, she stared at the mass of bottles and boxes in the dim dark shop which was full of the sight and smells of dried spotted toads, magic mushrooms, venom of purple spider, eye of the bat, old snakes' eggs, spit of black frog etc., which were crammed from floor to ceiling in this musty old shop. After what seemed like a lifetime, old Sagacious returned to the front of the shop some fifteen minutes later, and triumphantly handed over a large round package wrapped in red ribbon and placed it on to the dusty counter.

'Handle that carefully my girl. It's a sacred secret formula of Cubis Arvina from the time of Aristotle and Pompest the Modest in 350BC.' The old man gave her a conspiratorially half smile in encouragement.

Clastara could not thank the wise old man enough, and so she hurried back to the castle with her precious parcel clutched securely to her bosom.

Meanwhile, Prince Claude with great flourish had assembled the court and the servants in the throne room to witness Clastara's return and his dastardly- planned humiliation of her. Agnes the cook stood nervously to the side, looking anxiously out of the window at the moat that was rapidly filling up with acrid foul-smelling effluent. At the prince's behest, the royal guards were assembling in haste the ducking stool next to the drawbridge with the leather straps ready for the wrists and ankles of the next hapless victim.

'Now you useless girl, what have you brought for me? Remember, if you have failed me, you know what punishments awaits you, you worthless nobody! But if, you have brought back *exactly* what I instructed, then I will carry out my promise to personally clean and polish the castle from top to bottom.' Giving a smirk, his voice echoed around the room as if he was confident of the outcome that was steeped in his favour.

From behind her back, balanced on a crimson cushion, Clastara nervously handed the package over to one of the courtiers to be handed to the prince.

On seeing the brown package, the prince cocked an eyebrow in surprise. 'Um...' he said. 'Now what in royal heaven's name have we here?' His heart missed a beat as his eyes were drawn as though mesmerised to the neatly tied up package.

Because at that precise moment, he fervently hoped that inside the package was a jar of his favourite sweetmeats of honey and lavender drops, together with a polite note from old Sagacious countermanding the princes' extraordinary request for a specifically described potion of special grease, and furthermore his confirming that the product did *not really* exist…

However, tearing off the red ribbon, and carefully opening the package a large pot fell out much to the astonishment of the prince. A courtier picked it and dutifully handed it over to the prince as Agnes and Clastara fluttered their hands over their mouths in fear. On prising the lid open, the pot revealed a thick sludge of turgid green and yellow grease, which gave off a distinct odour of feline urine.

The prince gagged and almost fainted. Overcome with the pungent smell, he quickly thrust the pot back to his footman. Labelled clearly in bold letters on the side of the pot it described verbatim…

"Cubis Arvina" – by Royal Command of HRH Prince Claude the Languid. Herewith, a unique Royal formula of Elbow

Grease. To facilitate his Royal Highness to clean the Royal Kingdom as instructed in the letter."

'But…but. Wait a minute…*there's no such thing as elbow grea…!*' Sweating profusely, he started to protest vehemently.

Searching around him, his eyes pleaded with his courtiers and particularly Agnes the cook for support.

However, his plea fell on deaf ears. When Agnes gave a nod, the others followed suit as the indisputable evidence was right in front of their very eyes. Prompted by his audience, he dipped his fingers into the turgid smelly slime to take a small sniff at it to see if it was real, when he let out a gasp of horror, and collapsed into the arms of his astonished but loyal footman.

Apoplectic with rage that his ruse had backfired, he ranted and raged using what is deemed totally inappropriate and not very regal expletives that rang out through the castle that day. But however, such language cannot be repeated for publication or for posterity. Meanwhile, suffice to say that Prince Claude the Languid with the critical eyes of the whole kingdom watching, had no option but to roll up his sleeves, smear the elbow grease from his elbows to his fingers. Whereupon his whole frame contorted with fury and self-pity, sank on to his royal knees and set to work in the very act of scrubbing, scouring, and polishing on that illustrious day. That day the 1st April 1453 henceforth became known throughout the kingdom as Cubis Arvina Day.

(Later known in history as the Royal Reckoning Day)

Epilogue

And thus, the horrible fate of the young maid Clastara was duly mitigated. For soon afterwards, she left the castle to be an apprentice to wise old Sagacious at the Apothecary and ended up marrying his son, Ignatious the handsome sorcerer. As the years passed, she successfully learnt everything there was to know about magical and mystical potions – especially for e.g, elbow grease *– for which she had patented the secret formula, and from which she reaped the rewards of fame and fortune throughout the land. Even today, for the discerning connoisseur, one can still obtain a tin of it from obscure pharmacies and dispensaries in out-of-the way places around the globe. However, do look out for the all-important appendage… "By Royal appointment -" to guarantee that you are served the genuine article.*

THE ULTIMATE TAKEAWAY

Confronting his wife, he was adamant as usual that he knew the menu like the back of his hand.

'Don't nag me woman. I *know* how to order Chinese!' he blustered. 'They order by numbers.' In one quick movement he slipped on his jacket to face the frosty night air.

'Pig headed! Stubborn man…always knows best – just because he's an accountant!' she muttered under her breath as he made his way out of the door with the crumpled-up menu in his hand.

'And don't forget, my Sweet and Sour!' she shouted. 'But not too much of the onion!'

But he was out of earshot (or pretended to be) by the time he slammed the garden gate. Striding jauntily, he quickly reached the row of shops in the tiny parade at the bottom of the hill near to the village pub.

"The Blossom Garden" was the newly opened Chinese takeaway that took over from a dingy sandwich bar that had ceased trading five months ago.

"Free Prawn Crackers for orders over £15!" it advertised on the menu. *"Free Soft Drinks of your choice, for orders over £25 with free delivery,"* it boasted in a hand drawn poster taped across the steam-smeared window.

There were two other customers waiting before him at the counter, so begrudgingly he sat down on the padded bench next to the window to study last week's local paper and let out a groan. Looking at the sports page, he read with exasperation that the local team had lost again; this time hammered 6 – 1 at home.

'Bunch of useless amateurs!' he said, swearing into his upturned collar, 'My old granny could've done better with her ankles tied together!'

'Next, you – pleese…you like…e order?' called a slightly built Chinese woman in a tinkling voice that rose upwards in scale.

Gratefully, he jumped up and handed over his order – scribbled on a piece of paper – to whom he assumed was the cook and owner's wife. From where he and other customers stood, via an open door, he could hear pans and woks scraping and clattering furiously on a gas stove in a small kitchen at the back of the shop from where aromatic smells of "Char Sui" (that's Chinese barbecued pork to the uninitiated) heavily cloyed the air.

Fifteen minutes later, after drumming his fingers on the top of the counter and pretending to hum along with the strangled tune of the latest pop song that belted out from a small overhead speaker, a large white plastic bag was carefully and ceremoniously deposited on the top of the counter. Impatiently punching the code for his credit card, he picked up his order and started towards the door nodding gratefully to a customer who held it open for him.

'You like eat-ee nice Prawn Crackers and cola sir … no charge!' called the little lady after him in broken English in a pleasant sing song voice.

By now, dusk had fallen, and the streetlamps were lit, casting sharp shadows on to the grass verges damp from the falling mist. He puffed somewhat going up the slope of the hill in the direction of his house, blaming the weight of the cans of soft drinks, which he did not really need, but couldn't refuse as they came free.

'Home now, my dear!' he announced triumphantly as he kicked shut the front door. Impatiently, his wife sated with hunger, grabbed the plastic carrier her taste buds aroused at the smell of the Sweet and Sour Pork, Stir-fry Egg Noodles with Chicken, Chilli Beef and Special Fried Rice – a choice selection which she had previously ordered on a Saturday night, a fortnight ago.

As her husband drew up a chair to the dining table in hungry anticipation, he swept aside his knife and fork to be replaced by chopsticks, his wife opened the bag with a flourish. Opening the first container- yes, it was the Chicken noodles. Then it was followed by the Beef, and then the rice.

'Ah! Wonderful!' she remarked as she opened the next container with her favourite Sweet and Sour Pork. Then she pulled out another container that also had Sweet and Sour Pork.

They glanced at each other trying to stifle their surprise; her thinking that it was such a nice gesture that her husband had treated her to an extra portion of her favourite dish, and so she gave him a rare, but wry smile.

'But what on earth is this?!' As she pulled out a third container with a portion of Sweet and Sour, there was another: then yet another, followed by the same again. Staring at them, she eventually counted *thirteen* portions of Sweet and Sour Pork.

'What the damn devil have you done?' she screamed at her husband.

'But…but…hang on!' he huffed weakly, *'I didn't…order…'* his voice trailing away.

'Let me see that bill and a copy of your wretched order!' demanded his wife, jabbing her finger, her face contorted with increasing fury.

Sheepishly, he handed over a copy of the bill and the copy of the takeaway menu on which he had scribbled his order. Flattening the curled-up copies in the palm of her hand, she wiped away the grease that had splattered on them; then she slowly read out…

'Number 3: Chilli Beef x 1.

Um…

Number 5: Fried Egg Noodle with Chicken and special sauce x 1.

Number 8a: Special Fried Rice… Blossom Garden Style.'

'AND *the Sweet and Sour Pork'*…he interjected, full of self pity. 'I got what you asked for!'

'But **YOU'VE** ordered thirteen of them!' she screamed at him accusingly.

'No, I didn't…' he protested vehemently. Completely flummoxed, he scrutinised the mass of open containers that spread across the whole surface of their dining table. It was dominated by a mass of orange, glutinous sea of Sweet and Sour Pork Balls floating in onion and pineapple. The vinegary smell was overwhelming, infiltrating the room.

'Look you, stupid fool; you ringed and ordered No. 1: Sweet and Sour Pork x 13! Whereas you should've ordered **No. 13: Sweet and Sour Pork times 1** …. and not the other way round!'

Blood drained from his face. His jaw fell, open; but no sound came. For the next five days as a penance, he was forced to eat Sweet and Sour Pork with extra onions for breakfast, lunch, and dinner. He couldn't stand the sight and smell of sweet and sour for months thereafter. From that day onwards, he vowed that never again, would he arrogantly order with abandon from the top of his head. And furthermore, in future he would order, *meticulously* using *numbers*, (spelling out the quantity, for safety in his case) which is the method that the Chinese prefer.

The moral of this cautionary tale, is to always remember that the Chinese in their establishments have always for decades, for the benefit of the European customers, number their dishes on their menu from one (1) onwards…etc. Historically, it was originally for the sake of their kitchen as much as for the convenience of their waiting staff. Inanely it must sound, but even today, to avoid embarrassing and costly mistakes, you, the public are still advised to order strictly by numbers.

For example: "One portion of number 3. One of number 7" on the menu, and so on.

Because, with just one slip or a single mistake, you could end up with a dozen portions of the same dish, instead of just one portion of it that you really wanted. How do I know? Well, this has happened before in our defunct family business; and it won't be the last.

And furthermore, talking of cross purposes or something that may have been lost in translation; I am reminded of an instance in the old days, many moons ago, when my late father asked one of the catering staff to go out to the market and buy twenty lemons. The waiter came back with twenty melons. Such are the vagaries of life.

ARTHOUSE – AN EXHIBITION LIKE NO OTHER

A quarter past three could not come a moment too soon, as scores of children rushed excitedly into the hall to greet their family and friends. Impatiently, they had been waiting for weeks on end to show them their work, which they had been covetously working on for what seemed to them an eternity.

This was an art exhibition like no other. It was part and parcel of a major exhibition called Arthouse involving the whole of the borough of Richmond, lead by many resident professional artists and designers and other local institutions which opened their workshops for the public for that day.

But this was the *Big One*: the centrepiece at *their* school…on *their* patch…at *their* infant school; a primary school that trailblazed like no other.

'It's the most important part of your young life; if you are just four, five or six. And especially if you're a pupil at Shirland Primary,' said one parent to me with possessive pride, as she noticed that I was a stranger…a visitor… just an ordinary visitor- a mere simple observer. But what I didn't expect, was an exhibition of the like I'd never seen before, and especially from the hands of children of that young age.

As my wife dragged me around the place, albeit initially rather reluctantly, my eyes were dazzled from the hundreds of displays made up of paintings, collages, models and so on, covering every inch of the walls, floors, and ceilings. Hanging like washing lines were a myriad of patterns and shapes that portrayed people, animals, creatures – both real and imaginary, strung across the vast space of the hall like festival garlands in anticipation of a special celebration about to take place.

And that was not all; countless numbers of amazing and unusual design projects festooned the tables, presented by different classes, Cherry, Birch, Maple, Apple and so on, named so aptly following nature.

Sweeping around the corner, a massive stunning frieze, that encapsulated water, figures, plants and trees painted in vivid greens and blues met my eyes, that even the great master Monet himself would have been proud to call his own. But we must pinch ourselves to remind us that this was the work of children so young.

Young Toby Smith, tightly clutching onto the hand of his mother Judy grabbed my attention. Excitedly, he showed me the beautiful badge he had moulded out of clay. Captivated, he explained the process of carving the design by hand and baking it in an oven… 'Like a cake,' he added with considerable pride.

Hovering in the background not to be outdone, shy young Charlotte (so my wife later discovered her name), previously partly hiding behind her mother's skirt, suddenly emerged from behind it with growing confidence. She dragged my wife over to a nearby table display and pointed animatedly. A gigantic spider sculptured in plasticine slept languidly among a nest of insects and tiny beasts (so vividly described by Charlotte as if they were real) on a black cloth with dozens of other incredible creatures. 'These were made by friends in my class!' she announced proudly.

'But it's got too many legs for a spider,' I was about to say. Immediately my wife gave me a censorious look, so I bit my tongue. After all, this was *their world. A child's world!* A world of eternal fantasy. One fired by unimaginable imagination. Belief suspended. A world of endless beauty filled with goblins, elfs and fairies. And not least by mythical creatures…even, strange-looking spiders with too many legs.

Wait 'till they grow up I thought. They would soon realise that insects have six legs and spiders have eight, I protested pompously under my breath. Ah, but then I was not five or six years old anymore, reminded my wife scathingly. For this was their world – one of infinite charm that we as impatient adults, so quickly rush in a hurry, to make them grow up far too soon.

Near to the entrance to the hall, just then a tiny figure with short fair hair tied back in bunches pushing her best friend gently in front of her, cajoled us to look at a gigantic whale lolling in the centre of the room. A crowd of adults with their children in tow crowded around this enormous mammal beached there on the polished parquet.

'Look it's turning its head as it cries!' one child squealed with nervous excitement. Indeed, from beneath the twenty-foot whale, sounds of the seas and its haunting cries calling to us – we the ordinary landlubbers, their distant cousins on land.

'I bet that's a recording,' I murmured knowingly. To which my wife hastily kicked my foot to shut me up.

'Took us ages to cover its body with skin made out of paper, then we painted it grey and black!' piped up a lone voice from a slim young boy trying to explain to anyone in earshot who cared to listen. We were all intrigued.

'But what about those hundreds of footprints daubed in different coloured paint surrounding the body of the sprawled-out creature in front of us?' I asked puzzled.

'Ah but?' interrupted Miss Ying (who happened to be our daughter) – one of the teachers, suddenly stealing up behind us, 'that is symbolic and supposed to mean the…'

'Can't you see that!' snapped another young pupil with appropriate indignation, his hands on his hips.

'Of course,' I stuttered, trying to work it out. 'It's a long time since I was your age,' I offered by way of an apology for being a bit slow, hoping that would be accepted as a valid excuse.

Surrounded by her young charges from Apple class, our daughter – their teacher – and just plain *Miss* to them, rolled her eyes upwards. Not unexpectedly, grown up daughters often do this with a mixture of affection and exasperation at the slowness of their fathers. It was especially more poignant today of all days, for Father's Day was as it happens only two days away.

'Congratulations in getting this amazing display off the ground,' began my wife in offering her compliments to our daughter, learning that she was one of the prime movers behind it.

'Oh, it was a team effort from all the staff who worked their socks off!' replied our daughter as she airily brushed the remarks aside, just a little embarrassed.

'Come and see the wildlife garden Mister!' shouted a bunch of children from Maple Class. Like the children with the Pied Piper, but in a role reversed, they led the way, giggling with a toss of their heads. As we snaked out of the main building, we dutifully followed, gathering several other adults along the way. Brushing past the Pirate Ship – a colossus of a magnificent model which rose out of the edge of the playground on the left like Blackbeard's Ship from days of old, we hurried to the wildlife garden our curiosity at bursting point.

Hidden away behind a low gate and bushes, suddenly in front of us was this magic oasis of a children's secret garden, they could jealously call their own. Stepping through a winding path of large flat stones we found ourselves in a jungle of wildflowers, colourful plants, sprouting shrubs, bushes and trees; a heady mix of scents and smells to tantalise the senses.

To the right of the garden, a tiny kidney-shaped pond sparkled in the sunlight as the light summer breeze caused shudders of ripples that bounced off the surface of the water. Tall proud bullrushes, flame coloured poker plants and a mass of sprouting green aquatic vegetation interlaced into a natural screen around the water provided a homely habitat for the wild beetles, grubs, insects, and creepy crawlies (a word designated affectionately by the children) to survive in.

'We are hoping to attract dragonflies and ladybirds,' said Judy, Toby's mother crossing her fingers. But just then, a fat copper-coloured bumblebee buzzed across our path covered in pollen, and high in the distance a blackbird and a robin began to sing.

'Mm, what a wonderful aria!' murmured my wife, enraptured by it all. 'You know, you're lucky to be surrounded by so much of nature and right on your doorstep,' she added with undisguised envy.

Pushing up between the flowers and wild grass and skirting the footings of a tiny greenhouse built in the middle of the garden was a surprising display of spindly sculptures. Twisted in multi-coloured wire with brightly-painted plastic heads and intertwined with an assortment of laminated shapes and so on, was a display – richly alive in ideas, poking out from beneath the undergrowth. It prompted my wife and I to think that Chihuly's incredible glass sculptures recently dotted around Kew gardens must have inspired the children and their teachers; and why not? One couldn't get better than that.

Toby ran ahead of us. We discovered by and by, that his mother Judy and a group of enterprising parents and teachers were instrumental in bringing the garden into being, though she dismissed the achievement with a modest wave of the hand. Thoroughly absorbed, Toby was now flat on his stomach at the edge of the pond, and together with two of his friends they were pushing sailing boats crafted out of tin foil along the water. The boats scudded across the pond as if they were upon the open oceans. Well, in their young minds, it could have been the high seas filled with pirates and sunken treasure – their imagination running rife in a private world of their own.

Up to their elbows, hands deep, scrambling into the darkened waters full of bright green pond weed, young Toby was the first to scoop up a fistful of frog spawn to proudly show us. Wrists smothered in clinging weed, desperately wanting us to see it, he dangled the gelatinous mass under our noses. Ugh, I thought grimacing; but then the innocence of childhood had left me a long time ago. My daughter joked laughingly that I had grown squeamish in my old age, as Toby carefully put the frog spawn back into the water, informing me that they will be jumping frogs one day, in case I had forgotten.

Our eyes couldn't keep still for one moment. Wherever they looked, they were dazzled. Fluorescent brightly-coloured glow sticks shone from the bushes. Giant translucent teardrops hung from the trees. Fairy lights glowed from the hedgerows. Magical creatures carved in wire crept amongst the undergrowth and even a gigantic butterfly in all its brilliance was suspended from the branches of the mother of all trees – a magnificent oak tree, which sat imperiously near the centre of the garden like a magic protective umbrella. Under its shade was a circle of small wooden benches where classes often met to read and to hear stories… 'It instils a calming influence on the children,' so we were reliably informed.

And that was not all: for strung between the branches of this and those of ncighbouring tree to its left, was another incredible work of art. An enormous sheet of cloth, which was flag shaped, that appeared to float in mid-air like an artistic apparition. It was bursting with shades of all colours of the rainbow. Squiggles, crosses, and blobs of every shape imaginable leapt out at us in an abstract blaze of technicolour.

'The class haphazardly rolled soft balls dipped in paint all over the cloth,' explained our daughter, in a matter-of-fact voice, as if the children did that regularly everyday.

'Yes, we did! We had fun getting our hands glued with gooey paint,' chirped several children from Apple Class, gesticulating at the canvas excitedly.

An awful thought then flashed through my mind of what today's Health and Safety would have made of this. I shook my head with a *"What does it really matter!"* as I smiled admiringly at what I saw in front of me. The grins of unbridled joy on their faces were enough to quell any doubts that foolishly lurked unfounded.

That stunning work of art, original in its spontaneity, unique in its expression of freedom, and such a witness to its shared fun and joy could command a King's ransom at the Tate one day I thought as my imagination ran away with me. Of course, one could dream; but why not?

'Ooh, the Mayor came to see us today with his gold chain around his neck!' chorused a group of children jumping up and down with glee.

'Ah, but we've just met the MP from Parliament!' boasted another group, not wishing to miss out. 'And what's more, the local paper is going to write about us and make us famous!' they said, chipping in with a harmless gloat.

As we left the secret garden my eyes were drawn back to the Pirate Ship now on the right. I wondered if my creaky knees would stand a climb up onto its deck when the children weren't looking. Instinctively, my wife read my mind and wagged a stiff finger under my nose warningly, that the headmistress, however kind and tolerant would take a very dim view of it. 'The Head and her staff have got enough on their plates as it is busily keeping an eye on everything today,' reminded my wife. And so, I desisted.

Exiting the gate from the school grounds, you simply could not miss a remarkable ...no – a simply magnificent masterpiece staring at you. Words seemed inadequate to describe such a beautiful life size sculpture of Mother and Child hewn professionally from Portland Stone, sitting discreetly like a guarding sentinel under a large maple tree, which was in turn decorated with giant glistening mobiles. To us, it aptly sums up the wondrous joy this State Primary school, which seems to continue to defy the boundaries of pride and love. It continues to cement a special bond of belonging to parents, children and staff and all those connected with this happy place.

As we climbed into our car to leave, I reflected on the impact the work of these children had made upon us; and I'm certain that we were not the only ones that day. Today, we were privileged to have had a tiny glimpse into their world to revisit childhood, which at this place of learning these young pupils had been left to their most valuable human asset of all – *their imagination – their creativity...* stimulated and unfettered, each in their turn. Their pride of tactile achievement running through their hands coupled with that enlightening experience seen brightly through their eyes. It was a childhood to remember; a time to treasure.

No television, computer games, videos or i pads were in evidence today. They did not need them. As the greatest gift they have came from within themselves. It was one of fertile imagination; natural, as it was infinite. It was a salutary lesson that the young could teach the old so much, in reminding us about ourselves that we have so easily forgotten.

Yet, somewhere in the dim and distant past, I seem to remember hearing that art is like music to the ears. It was a test to challenge our thinking. It pervades our senses, stimulates our minds. It builds a framework of hunger for all subjects under the sun. Art it is said is like nectar to the brain, and honey to soothe the spirit. It gives expression to our limbs and vital, like fresh air to the soul of learning. And who am I, just a mere visitor today to their precious world to argue. Well, enough said. So, it's Amen to that.

THE MAD HATTER'S TEA ROOMS

'We'll soon lick this place into shape!' he said to his wife as they surveyed the scene of their new home with a mixture of anticipation laced with a bit of anxiety of the future ahead.

The Lewis's, Douglas and Carol had just returned home to where they once grew up in East Anglia having spent twelve years away in Douglas's last posting in the British embassy in Oman. The Fens, albeit flat as a pancake was a welcoming oasis of fields of sumptuous English greenery, sturdy trees of oak and weeping willow and creeping mist rising from the many waterways that threaded through the countryside like giant tentacles. But after enduring the parched dryness of the desert and the constant humidity of the Middle East, they did not complain.

They opted to settle in a small village not far from St Ives. To them, the peaceful setting in such a backwater of rural England was paradise regained. It was the tranquil views of rural beauty from the front of the black and white timbered building which was once an ale house in the Tudor period facing a lake that became the deciding factor when they bought the house from the local estate agents last summer. The large lake, home to graceful swans and belligerent Canada geese flowed into an estuary of the Great River Ouse via a lock, was spanned by an ornate Victorian bridge of bleached white timber which only added to the enchanted location.

Wychwood House with its slanting oak floors, lopsided low ceilings, and ill-fitting doorways, had been on the market for a couple of years or so they soon discovered, but that did not put them off. 'It needed some tender loving care to restore it to its former historical glory', offered the estate agent encouragingly. 'As well as extremely deep pockets', the agent failed to add.

The shop with its former use as an old-fashioned coffee house was perfect to convert into a quaint old tea shop. Confident that it would blend seamlessly in with the picturesque sixteenth century village with its surrounding area of natural beauty that attracted many visitors, especially, since Oliver Cromwell's birthplace was close by and it being the historic setting of the battles between the Roundheads and the Cavaliers of Charles I, they sunk every penny of their hard-earned savings and pensions into Wychwood House. And added to that, as the historic city of Cambridge being a hub for students and foreign tourists from all over the world being a mere twenty minutes away by road, they felt that their venture could not fail.

'Once we have finished, we could name it, *"The Mad Hatter's Tea Rooms!"* joked Douglas, teasing his wife after the play on words of Lewis Carol from *"Through the Looking Glass fame"*. His wife rolled her eyes and looked up to heaven in exasperation, as she always did whenever he plagiarised and inverted his wife's name in vain.

The three rooms above the shop were more than adequate for the two of them and did not need any structural work. Decoration on the wattle and daub on the cellulose board suspended between the blackened rafters in white emulsion was just the ticket to freshen up the décor with their simple sticks of furniture that had been held in storage after all those years away.

'I only wish that there was a bit more daylight coming through those tiny panes of that acid-etched glass,' grumbled his wife. 'I could just about live with the rugs sliding away on the sloping floor in our bedroom, and even hitting our heads on the dangerously low door frame, but not the door banging shut each time because of the slope!'

Indeed, the Lewis's had difficulty in pushing the bedroom door open, and to keep it ajar due to the sharp camber of some two-inch drop that veered away towards the landing which made the door slam shut each time they entered. The noise sounded like a bomb exploding which reverberated throughout the timber frame of the entire house. Douglas then had a brainwave. He stuffed a large sock with material, and using string he tied it around the edge of the door from the door handle outside to the handle inside.

'Eureka!' he exclaimed proudly. 'There'll be no more banging of the wretched thing against the door jamb due to gravity, day or night!'

It was after a couple of months of hard work converting the shop with the help of local tradesmen that something out of the ordinary happened. Whenever Carol prepared the table in the dining room, on more than one occasion, she thought she sensed a strong smell of flowers, redolent of autumn leaves. But this was the middle of March. It could not have come from an arrangement of flowers in the room as she did not have any on display as she suffered from allergies – particularly hay fever, and moreover, spring buds were now beginning to blossom in the small garden at the rear of the house which only made her nose run.

One evening, her curiosity got the better of her; and so, she called out to her husband, 'Douglas, can you smell something like an old fashioned, perfume such as rosewater or something?' She sniffed like a bloodhound around the room, up and down, and into every crevice making a hissing sound through her nose and clenched lips.

'Well not really,' he replied, his mind preoccupied from the end of the day's labouring with helping the builders in the renovation works.

When his wife persisted, he tried to humour her and conceded that there might be a pleasant smell, a bit musty, like beeswax in an old church; but he couldn't swear to it. When pressed, he thought that the smell was coming from the back wall to the right-hand side of the fireplace, which backed onto the coal cellar in the kitchen next door.

'You haven't been using floor polish on the flagstones have you my dear?' He asked, already knowing that the answer would be rhetorical; because at this moment in time, they could only use soapy water, rather than polish to keep the floors reasonably clean whilst building works were going on.

However, on one gloomy night as rain fell with a curtain of mist rapidly rising over the water in front of the house, Douglas was woken up by the bedroom door gradually opening with gentle swish. It was hardly audible. Peering over the top of the bedclothes, he reached for his glasses from the bedside table. But he was too late, the door closed quietly again. Silently turning the corner of his blanket, so as not to disturb his wife who was deep asleep in a gentle sonorous snore, he crept out of bed and padded to the door. Carefully pulling back the door handle which was covered at one end with the padded sock, he prised the door opened, and looked up and down the small narrow landing to the stairs. Nothing could be seen, although hardly any vision was visible as it was virtually pitch black for it was still early hours in the morning. He held a damp finger up in the air. There was not a whisper of a draught. It was a windless night despite the drizzling rain persisting in heavy sheets outside. In any case, he knew full well that it would require a hefty push from the outside of the bedroom door to open it against the upward slope of the floor.

After visiting the bathroom, puzzled that he might have been mistaken thinking that it was all a dream, he gratefully crept back into the warmth of the bed, noting from the bedside clock that it was three in the morning. Plumping up his pillow, he thought that he could vaguely smell a hint of rose petals wafting from the doorway. Cursing that he was imagining things, he pulled the blankets over his head and fell into a fitful sleep.

Two weeks later, the same thing happened again. This time as the door glided gently open to about halfway, he kept still as a ghost, somewhat petrified. But in fact, he was rather annoyed with himself for being a bit of a wimp, that he didn't dare to reach for his glasses to see properly in case he shattered the moment. As far as he could make out in the slit of light coming from outside of the window, nothing tangible could be seen. The door closed quietly on its hinges as silently as it did when it had opened just a couple of minutes ago. Glancing at the clock, it was three in the morning. Again, he rapidly checked to see if his wife was asleep, he got out of bed, prised open the bedroom door and scanned the landing. Again, nothing could be seen. He returned to bed, more curious than scared, and as he fell asleep, he swore that there was a definite smell of rose petals in the air.

At breakfast, the very next morning, peering over his newspaper Douglas thought that he had better tell his wife. For fear of worrying Carol unduly, he nonchalantly described what had happened in the dead of night as if it were nothing really to be alarmed about.

'Oh,' she said in a mouse-like voice, 'I've been meaning to tell you, that it's happened to me on three occasions. But I've been a bit frightened to tell you, in case you think I was going mad, or blame the wine or the brandy that we've been having at dinner!'

Shortly after Easter, as it happened, the local vicar from the little gothic church at the end of the village called upon them whilst doing the rounds to welcome new residents to the community. The Lewis's, now rather lapsed as churchgoers whilst living abroad for long periods of their married life, had recently began to attend services again, and started to get to know the friendly down-to-earth, vicar, the Reverend Henry Eastbury. Well, on that Saturday afternoon after inviting Mr Eastbury to take tea, Douglas took the opportunity to tactfully tell him of the unusual goings-on at the house.

The vicar got out of his chair and strode around the dining room and scratched the top of his greying temples as if in deep thought. 'Well, in the circumstances, all I can advise is that you do not really need to conduct a drastic exorcize of the premises. From what you tell me, they or the person's spirit are quite benign… and in my humble opinion, they are best left well undisturbed!' Then without prompting, he proceeded to tell them of the stories of other mysterious goings-on in the neighbourhood that occurred over the years. 'However, I must admit that several haunting images have been reported in the past.' And he chose his words carefully to describe what had happened to other parishioners in the vicinity.

'A couple living next to the old cemetery had reported frequent sightings of words scrawled on their living room wall that were told by experts, mimicked garbled writings from medieval times. Others reported of fossilised lumps of bread appearing on their doorstep that were thought to be several centuries old. Another resident at the edge of the village, near to the old Roman Road complained of a tall hazy figure appearing on his staircase, and when the bishop of the diocese came to try to exorcize the house, things got out of hand with furniture being hurled about, and then the privet hedge in the back garden spontaneously caught fire! Therefore, with due respect, I can only repeat my advice,' cautioned the vicar. 'Some things are best left alone; especially anything to do with the paranormal! But, however, if you are really interested, I'm reliably informed that the previous occupants of this house did carry out some research on this house's history many years ago.'

The Lewis's were intrigued with the story; but it was true to say, they were somewhat disturbed at the same time from what they were about to hear.

Mr Eastbury stood with his back to the fireplace and taking a crumpled white handkerchief from his trouser pocket, blew loudly and wiped his brow.

'From what I gather, in the Elizabethan period, something extremely sad happened on this very site. An aristocratic London lady, who once served in the court of Elizabeth I in the late fifteen hundreds lived here. And it was said that in the year of 1578, something tragic happened to her husband after he had failed to return home from a pilgrimage to Ely. His mount was found wandering aimlessly without its rider near a water meadow not far from here. Some say that she or her restless spirit kept on searching for him for the remainder of her days. Did she suddenly die of a broken heart or something else? Records fail to reveal what ultimately happened to him or her after the house was closed-up and sold on. This is hearsay, mind you. You can look this up in the archives in the public library in Cambridge.

But from what I do know, is that the previous owners of this house in the 1950's wanted to excavate the cellar behind your dining room wall to see if there were any mysterious clues left from the past or heaven forbid, find any human remains. But they were advised strongly against it by the local surveyor. He cautioned as to what might happen to the structural integrity of the building. And certainly, from the experience of my predecessors from the church, I would reiterate my advice. I would strongly suggest leave sleeping dogs lie if I were you. As far as I know, no one has suffered tragic consequences here, more than what I have already mentioned, or had been harmed. And this, if you allow me, nothing sinister has really happened to either of you. And this is extremely reassuring.' After that, the vicar respectfully took his leave after thanking his hosts for tea.

Soon afterwards, Carol and Douglas put it to the back of their minds and poured their energies in finishing the building works in readiness for the opening of their tea rooms. For following the vicar's visit, the couple did not have any further sightings or wafts of "fragrance" returning. Six weeks later as summer beckoned, their renovations were almost at an end. To celebrate, Douglas proudly asked his wife to sit in the inglenook in the large open fireplace they and their builders had painstakingly over the months excavated and now revealed to its former glory of yesteryear. This was to be the stunning centrepiece to their tea rooms.

Clutching a flute of champagne, Carol ducked her head under the large, blackened-oak beam that straddled the fireplace and sat on a stool on the left-hand side, inside the inglenook. Douglas instructed his wife to raise her glass as he focussed his shot with his polaroid camera.

One minute later, a photo began to roll out from the lip of the instant camera. In anticipation, Carol and her husband crouched over it expectantly.

But to their surprise and utter horror, the picture that had emerged into their hands was *not* a photo of Carol at all. With hesitant fingers, they examined the photo upside down, back to front, rubbed it vigorously, and even tried to peel it at the corners in case it had got stuck to another print by mistake. But clearly what was seen in the film, were two, yes *two, bulky and sinister looking figures* – one male and one female complete in what appeared to be in dark medieval garments sitting left and right of the inglenook. Douglas jammed the photo close-up to his glasses in disbelief. All he could see were featureless faces enshrouded by black voluminous cloaks and hoods; the female clutching what appeared to be a scraggy dead bird by the legs and the male holding a curved dagger in front of his throat!

Carol and her husband were stunned for a minute or two, their mouths opening and shutting like goldfishes gasping for air. They looked again. Then slowly and gradually as the ink on the photo began to dry, gruesome features on the figures began to materialise in detail. It started with a pair of hollowed-out eye sockets, spreading to a bloody gash to where their noses should have been. They let out a blood-curdling scream of terror as they dropped the camera and photo onto the floor like a hot potato and fled out of the house. Overcome with fright, they slammed the door with an almighty bang, vowing *never* to return.

Epilogue

Well, soon afterwards, the press descended on this humble village like an army of ants over a pot of honey, shattering what was hitherto a backwater of tranquillity. The photograph was taken away by a prominent member of the European Psychic Society. It was authenticated by a barrage of tests, even using carbon dating, and it was confirmed as being genuine taken in real time.

How do I know that this story took place? Well, I was a young reporter on the local paper at the time, and I found out that by sheer coincidence that my grandfather once lived at Wychwood House in the forties; and he too had disappeared near to the river across from the house in unexplained circumstances. His body was never found.

CHRISTMAS PRESENT

It was a cold and bitter night: typical of the time of the year, a day just before Christmas. Overhead the thick grey sky was overcast – pregnant with snow bursting to fall again over the little picturesque village which was tucked away and hidden amongst the jutting hills of the Pennines. The continuous blanket of snow on the grass verges was only broken by a lone figure of a man trudging his way methodically towards a small grey stone house about half a mile in the distance at the foot of the village. With a brisk sweep of his glove, he brushed the snow that had peppered his head from the time he had walked the last couple of miles from where the bus had dropped him on the main road. Cursing under his breath that he was a fool not to have remembered to bring a hat and a thick coat when he landed at the airport five hours earlier. Pulling up his collar and breathing hard to keep his face warm from the biting wind, he stamped his feet deliberately with each step of the way in an effort to feel his toes. Looking up through the approaching gloom, he wondered what he would do once he reached his destination. The borrowed light from the front window beckoned him on, illuminating the tiny path in front of the house like a reassuring beacon of encouragement.

Inside the warmth of the house, three young children were fervently busy, adding decorations to the tree and hiding the presents amongst the sparkling strands of silver tinsel strewn around the floor. Lucy, the eldest, who was nine, hovered over the dining table as she carefully pushed two red candles through the sprigs of holly sitting around the crimson blooms of the poinsettias and jammed them securely into the soil below. Deep in the kitchen amongst the steam and the heat from the oven, Katy – her mother, with considerable effort heaved a roasting pan heavy with a ten-pound turkey over to the sink to baste off some of the fat. Leaving it to cool on the side of the draining board, she lifted an oven-gloved hand towards her face and instinctively pushed back some stray strands of blonde hair with the back of her arm. She rubbed a gap in the oil-filled steam that had clung to the windows. Just then she gazed disconsolately out of the window, not really focussing on the bleak darkness and lonely silence that stared back at her, and which had enveloped the house locking her and her children within. She looked down at the turkey, jabbed at it distractedly with a fork and realised inexplicably that she had started to cry.

The man struggled on with increasing effort as he headed towards the village. In his left hand he carried a large holdall, which bulged at the rim; if it was heavy, it did not show. His arms hardly moved as he walked robotically on with his eyes concentrating in front of him, his jaw set with determination. No biting wind amidst the snow flurry that had just fallen would divert him from his task. As he got nearer, his step slowed, becoming stealthier by the minute. Relief came over him on seeing that no neighbours were around in case they thought that he was a stalker.

Katy and the children were sitting cross-legged on the floor around the Christmas tree fussing with the decorations. Through a gap in the curtains, he watched as she fiddled with the tiny lights, her face set in a frown of concentration. His eyes drunk to their fill the curves of her body, and all at once he felt an overwhelming desire which he tried to control. Shaking his head, he slipped past the wisteria clad walls – now shorn of leaves – to the back of the house facing the kitchen. Suddenly he became aware of the heat inside and how very cold and tired he was. He reached a numb hand towards the kitchen door, cautiously turned the handle, and felt it give way. Carefully stepping over the threshold, after scraping his shoes on the mat, the enticing smell from the oven now flooded his senses. A sudden hunger and a desperate longing overcame him and made him gag. Gently, he put the bag down on the white tiled floor and turned to close the door when he detected a movement out of the corner of his eye and swung around. Katy stood there like a statue. A scream started to rumble from the back of her throat. She clamped a hand across her mouth.

The door from the dining room started to open behind her. 'Go back inside Lucy. Now!' she barked at her daughter and the door closed again. *'What do you want?'* she demanded.

For a moment, he hesitated. He moved a step closer to her; his tall athletic frame filled the small kitchen. 'I want to come home, Katy. I *want* to come home.'

All the pain that had swum around in Katy's head for so long flooded up all at once like a knife, and she spat at him, *'Well, we don't want you.* We've learned to manage just, fine without you! So, you can just take your damn wanderings – with God knows who…with your lame excuses and long absences. So therefore, get the blazes out of here!'

The man literally shrank back; not so much from the words, but from the venom with which they were uttered. 'I'm sorry. I'm *really,* sorry,' was all that he said. Suddenly, he felt that he had no right here; not even to see his children. Wracked with remorse, he bent to pick up his bag to leave.

'Daddy!' the two younger children rushed through the door and threw themselves at him. He turned to hug them, enclosing them possessively inside the safety of his coat and saw that Lucy now stood silently besides her mother, unsure. The man unzipped the top of the bag which stood open on the floor besides him. It was full to the brim with presents, all wrapped in silver paper with red ribbons and large bows. He removed the first one. 'I got this especially for you, Lucy,' and held it out towards her like a peace offering. She reached out her hand, and he grabbed her and circled her with his arms. As she leant against his chest, he stroked her hair and laid his cheek on her head. A lone tear fell from her eyes. 'Daddy, Daddy!' the little boy and his twin sister tugged at his coat, 'You've got to put the Christmas presents under the Christmas tree!'

The man looked at his wife, who knew at once she was lost from the moment she saw him. 'Why don't you take your coat off,' she said with weary resignation. 'I can't get the blasted fairy lights to work.'

'I'll make it work,' he said. 'I promise you. *I'll make it work.'* And they all left the kitchen and went to see the tree.

(Inspired by and dedicated to Stephanie Curtis – with an invitation to contact the writer)

A DIVISION OF SPOILS

When I was nine or ten, I had a friend named Colin who being a couple of years older than me was rather intrepid and was regarded as the leader of our gang. There were a couple of other boys that hung around with us; Johnny Hughes, a coal miner's son, and Barry Steen from the local cobbler's shop. Together we were loosely called the Gang of Daredevils. For instance, Colin had climbed the tallest tree in the nearby woods to get at a crow's nest for its elliptical-shaped, khaki-coloured, eggs. And last winter, we scaled the tall fence over at the Erdigg's estate belonging to Squire Yorke, when Johnny helped himself to a small Christmas tree for his widowed mother, only to be shot at by the irate gamekeeper. Allow me to explain. At the time, I lived in North Wales on the border of England with my family in a place called Wrexham, Flintshire as it was known then in the '50's. Wrexham was strategically placed as a hub in the centre of a sprawling spider's web with villages and suburbs radiating outwards with coal mining and farming at its core.

One cold October day when the leaves of autumn started to turn a golden hue, as usual there was nothing much exciting happening in this sleepy town, until Colin noticed that a rather grand funeral was taking place under our noses. From the western outskirts of town, where there were some magnificent houses for the richer folks, a glass-sided hearse containing a handsome coffin, drawn by four fine horses slowly trotted into view up the hill towards us. A tall thin man dressed in a long black, frock coat and top hat in all its finery, walked at a snail's pace in front of them, ostentatiously twirling a silver tipped cane leading the dirge of a procession. Two of the horses were coal black and the other two dapple white, with plumes of tall white feathers strapped regally to the crowns of their heads. Two footmen, also decked in black, their top hats having a white silk bandana wound around the rims, and with white gloves stiffly holding the reins taut to the bridles, the horses pulled at a slow and mournful pace. Only the odd sound of the horses whinnying broke the respectful silence.

The clip-clop of the horses' hooves rattled on the cobblestones like striking sharp flint. It echoed around the increasingly dull grey sky as three black limousines full of solemn mourners followed, making up the cortege and which was packed with white blooms and wreaths on the roofs of the vehicles. The pavements were dotted with people, silently watching curiously, their hats and their caps clutched solemnly in their laps.

'Let's follow where they are going!' whispered Colin into my ear, beckoning to the other two friends with the crook of his finger.

Twenty minutes later, the cortege swept through the gates of the ancient cemetery, the back of which was next to our school. What was striking about this cemetery was that it had fallen into disrepair a long time ago. The large old wrought iron gates, rusty and black were falling off their hinges, and the graveyard was full of ancient headstones which were encrusted in moss and orange lichen, and most of them twisted at odd angles or had collapsed completely in a broken heap like the occupants that were lying peacefully underneath. Neglected was the word that Colin had aptly used. The old chapel, which must have been hundreds of years old, was largely derelict and with just the four walls standing after the roof had caved in. With only pigeons roosting in the eves, and the wood-rot door – damaged beyond repair as well as the leaded windows smashed over the years, probably by vandals, it looked a sorry sight. The smell of rot and decay hung in the air.

But to one side of the cemetery, with the use of a small, temporary building – having special dispensation from the bishop of the diocese, occasional burials could still take place in family graves, and that section of the churchyard was reasonably well looked after, for the grass verges were tended to from time to time. We assumed that is where this grand cortege was heading. As the last limo followed the hearse slowly into the grounds, Colin stuck out his arm and we stopped abruptly at the gates, for we didn't dare follow the cortege further as we stuck out as nosy intruders.

'Look. Let's come back much later, when it's dark!' challenged Colin, bordering on the foolhardy, if not dangerous. Askance, Johnny Hughes and I looked at each other, a smell of fear radiating from our faces.

'I dare you to explore the graveyard at night. I've been longing to see inside the old chapel when it's really, pitch black!'

'Heh! You're not scaredy cats, are you?' mocked Barry Steen, shrugging nonchalantly.

'Nar. Course not!' I said, putting on a brave face.

'That's arranged then. Let's meet at seven the corner of the street, next to the school wall, the bit which divides the cemetery from the school,' said Colin.

I stared briefly at Johnny, my eyebrows raised, eyes widened, and reluctantly nodded.

At the appointed hour, the four of us met. Pushing open the gates, which groaned on the hinges, Barry hissed, 'Lads, just stick together. But run like hell if a copper turns up, or we'll be for it and be in front of the beak in the morning!'

Proceeding in a line like devoted acolytes, I followed Colin who led the way into the cemetery using his mum's battered old torch, whose Eveready batteries were about to give out. I struggled to keep up with the rest of the gang who were much bigger than me.

'Heh. Look at this old headstone,' said Colin, shining the dim torch light onto one of the old graves. 'It says, "Mavis Knowsley. RIP. Born 1814, died 1872 of tragic consumption."'

'That's TB', I said knowingly.'

'Swot head!' retorted Johnny glaring at me in the dark.

Suddenly, there was a yelp that shattered the eerie silence a few yards behind us. We turned our heads and rushed back along the path from where we had come, our hearts in our mouths. Colin quickly shone his torch in front of him, searching. Barry, being short sighted had tripped over a broken piece of headstone which was leaning precariously at right angles, and he had fallen down a hole next to it. With Herculean effort, using his armpits, Johnny and I tugged like mad and dragged him out. Angrily, he brushed down his trouser legs and shoes now sodden with clumps of soil and damp moss.

'My mum will kill me with ruining the only pair of shoes I've got!' moaned Barry. 'I slipped on a slimy old grass snake by accident,' he added sheepishly, as if that was a valid excuse.

Negotiating a side path to the right, the old chapel building loomed ahead of us, casting a long shadow from the beam from the torch.

'Now gang! Who's brave enough to go through that old door?' asked Colin, waving the torch provocatively.

The rest of us didn't say a word. I stared at the ground my lips clamped shut.

'Okay you chicken livered lot. As the leader, *I'll* go in first and then you lot have got to follow!' offered Colin full of bravado.

With that, he pushed open the old timber door which creaked and moaned as he stepped cautiously inside.

No sooner had he entered the building, Colin leapt out again with a terrified scream, his hands fluttering around his head, slapping his hair in horror. 'Urgh! Yuk. Flying bats. Disgusting!!'

Then, no sooner had we approached the back wall of the graveyard next to the school, we suddenly heard low muffled voices that seemed to come from near to the slabs of old headstones that were stacked neatly against the wall under a row of mature horse chestnut trees. We stopped dead in our tracks as balloons of mist from our open mouths froze in the chilly air in front of us. Colin held a finger to his lips to signal for us to be quiet.

'Did you hear that?' he asked nervously.

We all shook our heads.

We listened hard, against the stillness of the night that you could cut with a knife.

We heard it again. This time, more distinctly.

'One for you, and one for me! …The fresh new ones just fallen are always the best! So, it's one for you and one…'

'Oh, my g-god!' I uttered out aloud. *'It's God and the Devil sharing the spoils!'*

'Flippin' hell!' screamed Colin. 'That new corpse earlier *must've* just been claimed and carved up already!'

For a minute or two, we looked at each other in the dim torchlight, scared witless, our hearts pounded like mad in our chests. Then we flew out of the cemetery as fast as our legs could carry us and ran all the way home, vowing never to go to the cemetery again.

Epilogue

The very next day at the school, two pupils had been hauled in front of the Head for trespassing over the cemetery wall at night time when raiding the horse chestnut trees for conkers. They admitted to the Head, that all that they were doing was quite harmless and were simply dividing the spoils of conkers equitably between them. Nevertheless, sharing they did, for they in turn shared six of the best.

"One for you, and one for me…One for you and…!"

THE FIRST LESSON

'Since you're eighteen, it might be a good idea if you learned to drive,' said my father, when I returned home from university for the long holiday. Generously, he offered to pay for a course of lessons with his former driving teacher, Roger Cummings who had started a successful driving school of his own after working for some years for a well-known national driving organisation.

It was the beginning of that hot summer, when I first met Roger. He turned up to collect me from the family home in an astonishing new car, called a Ford Consul. It was a 1960 model, and it was considered in my teenage eyes, a bit "flash". It was maroon with elongated fins at the rear in white, "rakish" my mates would call it when I later described it. Rather like its owner I thought at the time. Roger was tall, and what the ladies would call had a roguish charm about him. I think he was in his early thirties. Sandy haired, with twinkling eyes, he would grip a cigarette skilfully in his mouth, when at the same time smile and bark out instructions through his surprisingly white teeth.

'Turn right. Hand signals! Slow down. Watch that, Zebra!' as he controlled the speed of the Ford using dual controls.

It was in the aftermath of the second lesson that I discovered Roger's modus operandi. He would cut short my lesson by some ten minutes, when tactfully complimenting me on my swift progress in getting up to fourth gear on reaching thirty miles per hour. Then he would drop me off at a coffee bar on the other side of the city to enable him to collect his next pupil. Idiotically, I didn't raise much objection at the time which I should've have done in retrospect as it meant getting a long bus journey home. Until by chance, I discovered that his next pupil was a petite busty brunette at whom Roger ogled hungrily like a cat who got the cream. Once, slap in the middle of one lesson, Roger asked me to drive out to a dilapidated suburb of the city, where on the pavement outside a block of unremarkable flats, stood a tall redhead, heavily made up and reeking of overpowering perfume.

Teetering on three inch-stilettos, she slid into the rear passenger seat, her tight leather skirt making an odd slurping sound as it skidded on the hide-covered seat.

'Say hello to Madeleine,' urged Roger nonplussed, grinning lasciviously from ear to ear. 'She'll be gaining some extra experience by riding with us novices before her lesson starts.' Extraneous mileage he obsequiously called it.

Not long afterwards, on another occasion, Roger called at his house on the other side of town in order to collect messages, to see if there were any alterations in his bookings for the rest of the day. That is when I met Cathy, his wife. Tall and willowy, just like her husband, but Cathy must have been a few years younger than him and had kept her girl-like figure with her love of ballroom dancing and jogging with their cocker spaniel Flo according to Roger.

'Why hello!' she purred, as she offered a slim hand with long nails painted crimson. 'You must be the new young man studying science up in Newcastle, I hear.' Disconcertingly, she was one of those striking natural-blonde creatures with ice blue eyes who would stare directly, close into your face as if you were the exclusive centre of her attention. Later, I discovered that it was because she was extremely short sighted. And just like me, through vanity, refused to wear her glasses in public, particularly, if she wanted to impress someone she wanted under her spell. Much later, it had struck me, why someone like her erstwhile husband would want to sample a boring old ham sandwich outside of the house when he already had a delicious banquet with sumptuous delicacies waiting for him at home. The human mind boggles at the illogic of the errant male.

Anyway, I had met Cathy on a couple of occasions when her husband stopped at home for a cup of tea and a break during a lesson. In our animated conversation, I found out that she was a schoolteacher at the grammar school, teaching music and amateur dramatics. Furthermore, it was revealed that she revelled in the company of young people teaching dance as a form of exercise.

However, I digress. It was on one dreary Sunday morning, when my father shouted to the top of the house to say that there was a call on the phone asking for me. After getting up rather late, irritably, I rushed down to the phone which was in the hallway. 'Yup… Speaking.' I replied.

Puzzlement was quickly replaced by astonishment, when the caller with the husky voice from which I immediately worked out was Cathy Cummings, although she failed to mention her name as such. The conversation, I must say, was quite bizarre by any stroke of the imagination.   By and large, it was predominantly one way; she chatted as if taking on a persona of a third person with some incidental revelations about herself.

'The slow foxtrot is a favourite, followed by the rumba a close second. Do you dance by the way?'

Before, I had time to reply, she flitted from one subject to another, such as the intricacies of oriental cooking, or on how the summer heat made her unbearably hot, and that she must get some cotton dresses from Bon Marche and as well as some really, thin nightwear from Dorothy Perkins. After a few minutes of this inane conversation, I distinctly heard in the background, a door opening and then shutting, coupled with a dog barking. She suddenly stopped in midstream, cupping the earpiece, for the volume of sound became muffled,

'Oh, it's you darling; won't be a moment,' she shouted deliberately over her shoulder (one can only assume). 'It's one of the parents asking about the exam results!' Promptly, she then put the phone down with a purposeful click.

Well, this extraordinary turn of events happened twice again. Again, on a Sunday morning, a similar one-way, conversation ensued much to my continuing amazement. Oh, in the middle of this intrigue, I forgot to mention that I had phoned a girlfriend named Patsy whom I had met at college, and I asked her opinion of how the feminine mind worked. Patsy warned me in no uncertain terms that Mrs Cummings was playing a clever game. And I had to be extremely careful otherwise I could be flattened in the middle of a drama with its competing plots that were poisonously laced with sexual innuendo between a husband and wife. But then it occurred to me that the female species was streets ahead of the poor naïve males, such as us.

I thought there and then that I had worked it out. Well just about. Three weeks later, there happened to be a dinner dance at my father's city restaurant to celebrate The Dragon Boat Festival. Like previous events such as the Chinese New Year, the evening was commercially a great success, being fully booked. Roger and his wife were invited. And after the polite introductory small talk, I noticed that the two of them were behaving like young lovebirds as if on their first date. Dancing intimately close together in the waltz, they whispered sweet nothings in each other's ears, nuzzling like teenagers into the other's shoulders.

What was galling, was that Cathy virtually ignored me all evening, even when she bumped into me at the bar. Not one reference was made to the strange and overtly flirtatious telephone calls she had made to me in the past month or so. I shrugged it off, thinking I could never understand the inscrutable mindset of glamorous women a decade or so older than me. I suppose unfairly, I made a sweeping generalisation that they were on a different planet to us modern eighteen-year-olds. And so, I dismissed the tantalising overtures completely out of my mind. *Well almost.*

Just before I was due to return to Newcastle to the sanctity and sanity of people of my own generation, Cathy called; this time early one Thursday evening. You can imagine my surprise. An alarm bell rang in my ears, but I chose to ignore it. I was intrigued, as this could be the last throw of the dice. She said that she would like to see me before I return up north and would I like to join her to see the latest Albert Finney film, "Saturday Night and Sunday Morning," on at the Odeon in the centre of town, and perhaps share a last coffee together. Before I gasped out my reply, she murmured conspiratorially,

'Oh, in case you're wondering, R's away for the weekend, Meet me outside the box office at seven on Saturday. Don't be late!' She added firmly as though I was one of her pupils.

Saturday evening couldn't come a minute too soon. I carefully pressed my one and only suit; it was a plain worsted in charcoal grey from Burtons. I fussed over my striped-purple tie and white poplin shirt from C & A's, and I cleaned my teeth vigorously and tested my breath by blowing into my cupped hands. Smoothing down my rebelliously spiky hair, I scrutinised my image in front of the bathroom mirror. Satisfied, I thought that the person grinning sardonically back at me would pass muster. A tinge of excitement over the unknown overcame me which reminded me of my first date. Allowing plenty of time, I picked up a small box of Cadbury' Roses from the corner shop on the way and with a spring to my step I leapt onto the number 13 into town full of anticipation, if not with unreasonable expectation.

Like in the movies, to allow me time to make a grand entrance to impress my date, I planned to stop at a street well ahead to the front of the cinema, as the bus would normally go past the planned rendezvous by a couple of streets or so.

Suddenly the bus stopped at the crossroads where there were traffic lights, so I jumped off. About two hundred yards in the distance, I could just make out on the pavement outside the cinema walking ponderously up and down in the evening gloom was the unmistakable figure of Cathy wearing a dark trench coat with a fetching headscarf. She was smoking a cigarette, nervously glancing around her, warily. Taking off my glasses and stuffing them into my top pocket, I increased my pace in eagerness along the dark pavement towards her – bumping blindly into several passers by, when on reaching what was probably shouting distance to her, a car suddenly appeared. Accelerating at speed from a side road next to the cinema, it pulled outside the waiting Cathy with the engine running. The passenger door flew open as if from an invisible hand. My mouth ran dry, as immediately, I recognised the unmistakable maroon Ford Consul belonging to her husband Roger. Choking with fury, I spun on my heels and reversed abruptly in an about-turn to disappear amongst the swathes of humanity walking in the opposite direction.

With my heart thumping like mad, and in case I had been spotted, I walked quickly away, only to glance over my shoulder to see Cathy jump into the car as it roared away with its tyres squealing. On the way to the bus stop I angrily flung the box of chocolates into the nearest bin and kicked the lamppost in frustration of what might have been.

I didn't manage to complete my driving lessons. However, the amazing thing that came out of this extraordinary interlude during my college holidays, was that I managed to pass my driving test at first go. Some ten months later, I heard through my parents that the Cummings's had separated having sold up and that the husband had moved abroad. What became of Cathy, I wanted to ask; but then I thought better of it.

Eight eventful years then passed. Whilst working in London, I was lucky enough to marry a stunning fair-haired wonder, and my tuition in the artful complexities of the female psyche began. Caroline, a successful fashion designer was extremely sophisticated, having travelled abroad to many places, and wise beyond her years, she appeared to unravel the convoluting wiles of the female sex. On recounting the story of my misspent youth to my incredible and ever patient wife, who then explained that I had a lucky escape, for unwittingly, I might have been made a sacrificial lamb in the climax of that dangerous game in the battle of the sexes. I was told that it could have had disastrous, if not with fatal consequences, not only to me as a third party, but also between the couple themselves. For when both, I suspect led on the face of it sad unfulfilled lives. And particularly with the woman, who not only continued to mourn her lost youth, but similarly persisted in her fantasy as a "femme fatale" in desperately seeking male attention drawn to her web. Then, adding to this incendiary mix was an egotistic, weak-willed man whose sole preoccupation was to continue to ape Casanova and seemingly to the world was an abject failure and one who never grew up.

But to my eternal annoyance at the time, I never did discover the truth behind this enigmatic woman's brief, and what could only be described as more than a flattering interest in me in that blazing hot summer long ago. Did it really happen? Or was it a latent schoolboy's fantasy that was blown up out of all proportion at the time in an impressionable young mind, as well as in the misguided hope for bragging rights? The answer would bug me to my grave. As my glorious wife and long-term muse would say, that time in 1960 was probably my first real lesson in life in the coming of age.

THE HITCH

'Excuse me young sir. You don't happen to be heading for the old smoke, are you?' enquired a flat nasal voice from the side of the road. I leant over the passenger seat to stare at a lone figure of a man looking a bit tired from waiting for a lift. A quick look at the person indicated that on the face of it he looked harmless enough. In my judgement, he looked as if he was in his early thirties or so. He was about the same height as me, about five foot seven; slim, so if there were any problems along the way, I was arrogant enough to think I could deal with him, especially since I always kept an iron wrench handy under my seat. For self-protection, I hasten to add.

I'd better explain, this was the early sixties, and it was considered relatively safe to pick up needy hitch hikers in those days. Mind you, my parents would kill me if they ever found out. Moreover, wise older heads would *never allow* one's daughter to thumb a lift or to stop for hitch hikers for all the tea in China, whatever their sob story.

The man cocked his head to one side more in hope than expectation. I relented. 'Hop in then,' I said. 'And don't forget the belt.' (It was a simple single crossover Britax). At least if the individual was securely strapped in, not only in the interests of safety, but if push came to shove, then he'd have a job hijacking the car. It was reassuring if nothing else.

A gruff thanks followed as the crumpled stranger slipped into the passenger seat on his well-worn rayon trousers that did not match the old nondescript jacket he was wearing. And furthermore, in my opinion he could do with a decent shave having the remnants of an unruly beard.

'Throw your bag behind the seats,' I said, as I engaged the car into first gear to pull away. I acutely observed that it was an old khaki-coloured kitbag of the kind that soldiers once used. In my mind, he must have been an ex-serviceman. And that made it a whole lot better and placated my conscience by justifying my good deed for the day.

'Nice motor you've got son!' Unsolicited familiarity soon replaced the initial "sir", I thought sourly, as if the stranger had now rapidly changed into a pre-invited guest-passenger in those quick few minutes. 'Got proper leather seats these MG sports jobs,' he added making conversation as he stroked the seat affectionately with the flat of his hand.

'It'll take about twenty minutes to reach the beginning of the M1,' I said to distract him from embarking on anything more personal. 'This dual carriageway on the A45 meanwhile is the main access to the mouth of the motorway,' I announced airily, as I put my foot down on the accelerator.

'I bet this machine can rev to a ton in a blink of an eye!' said the passenger, as he slumped into the seat making himself at home. I turned on the radio to the Home Service in the hope that the passenger would soon fall asleep, and that all extraneous conversation would subsequently cease.

However, it didn't have the desired effect I thought it would, for he continued to burble on inanely – the subject matters not only unwelcome but superfluous. Gratefully, the car gobbled up the miles and we soon reached the beginning of the M1 passing the Blue Boar service station in a flash. Inwardly, I gave an inner sigh of deep regret for my generosity as there was still ninety odd miles to go. It was going to be long couple of hours I thought anxiously as an articulated lorry and several cars thundered past.

Just then my passenger sat up bolt upright, as if he had suddenly woken up from a snooze. 'Heh son.' (My title had now again denigrated as he addressed me patronisingly as "son", much to my ire). 'Do you see that HGV whizzing past, I bet he's carried some illicit cargo across the Channel in his time!'

He then plied me with statistics on the percentage of HGV's, mainly foreign who smuggled contraband, such as cigarettes and spirits to avoid purchase tax or duty. He must have noticed my exasperation at what was opined. My head jerked leftwards to see him tap the side of his nose conspiratorially as though he had some inside knowledge.

'And look at that old bloke with a flat cap over his eyes, hunched over his steering and speeding like a bat out of hell!'

I glanced out of the driver's side to see an old Morris Minor tearing past at eighty.

'Them old duffers think they're blinking Stirling Moss when they get behind the wheel!'

I must say that I was rather relieved when we reached halfway down the motorway when he suggested that we could stop for a break. I knew the Fortes Service station quite well from previous journeys.

'Can you get me a nice cuppa – three sugars, whilst I visit the necessary? Thanks squire!' My title had now been elevated up a notch somewhat, whether I really approved of it or not.

When he returned, he pulled up a plastic chair with a loud squeal of the legs, he started to roll a cigarette deftly using a finger and thumb on his right hand. I have to admit, it was a skill I admired, even though I wasn't a smoker. I was glad that he didn't offer me one, as I did not want to appear disapproving or old fashioned with an abject refusal.

With his rollup firmly clamped between his crooked teeth, he blew loudly on the steaming cup of tea, whilst I quietly sipped on my lukewarm coffee. It seemed strange that there was an audible silence for a minute or two as he concentrated on his drink. It didn't last long. Raising his head, he deliberately made eye contact. Oh – oh, I suddenly thought. Here comes the inevitable question on what my job was, and then the thorny subject of money! To my surprise and to his credit, he did not ask.

Then without prompting, 'you, young'uns starting off in life need to wise up in this rat race-world of ours. Always be savvy. Suss who's around you or behind for your own safety and the like!' he lectured. I wondered what was coming next, so I didn't comment. He continued rambling on without drawing breath. Wild horses couldn't stop him in midstream.

'You see them two blokes at the table at the back of the caff. Wait. Don't turn round, obvious like!' he hissed under his breath. 'Just swivel your eyes son. (It was now back to "son", as if reverting to type). They're coppers. Off duty!'

I raised my eyebrows quizzically.

'You can always tell. Their ties are never done up to the top. And the top button's I guarantee, nine times out of ten – undone. Their suits always seem too tight for them!'

Although I must confess that if these were the defining characteristics of our inimitable police force, then I really couldn't see it.

'Yours truly can smell the fuzz a mile away!' he added by way of further explanation. Disconcertingly he tapped the tip of his nose again.

My heart started to thump in a gasp of panic. In a transient moment of fear, my thoughts began to run away with me. Irrationally, I thought that I must have picked up a villain on the run.

As if he suddenly read my mind, he turned to me and said, 'relax, old son. I'm *dead* harmless.' This was followed by a crooked smile to reassure me. 'I mean. Just look at yours truly. Do I look like a bad 'un?' His increasing nasal tone and snippets of his phraseology suggested that he was probably a Londoner; perhaps from Kent or even from the borders of Essex to be generous.

'I mean. Me, I'm just a plain – Bob's yer uncle – a typical nobody. I mean young fella, could you hand on heart say you'd recognise me again if we bumped into each other in the street, or heavens forbid, finger me in a court of law.'

He offered a profile, and then facially front on, as if taking part in an identity parade. 'You see, if I shaved off this week's worth off my face with a sharp Gillette and got a regular short back and sides, I could be lost in a crowd like thousands of others.'

To be honest, he was probably right. He had no distinguishing features. He had sandy or perhaps mousey-coloured haired. A narrow face: Anglo Saxon or loosely described as English in appearance with a featureless nose and thin lips. And for all intents and purposes you could say that he was ordinary looking. Although if you wanted to nit pick, you would say that he was completely nondescript like millions of others in this country.

I suddenly went quiet.

'You see. I'm dead right, aren't I?'

I began to feel uncomfortable at being scrutinised like a bug under a microscope. Heat began to rise under my collar and tie.

'For instance, *you,* my son, would stick out in a crowd…with your smart clean looks and nice smart clothes! And with your typical Queen's English.'

My mouth began to open in protest that it was hardly a fair comparison. After all, relatively speaking that being ethnically Chinese, it was probable that I would stand out in a crowd – despite being born and bred here.

He went on. He jabbed a thumb in the direction of the car park. 'Yours a striking looking car for example – a bit obvious, I'd say in my learned opinion. Especially in flaming red! If you wanted to melt into the background, my old son, get a regular saloon; an ordinary bog standard four-seater. Like a Ford. And I'd advise dark blue. Don't bother to clean it – especially around the number plates. That way you could get away with blue murder if you wanted to.'

Stunned, I wanted to protest loudly that anything bordering on criminality was never in my scheme of thinking, never mind ever contemplating the heinous act of murder. To end the conversation, I abruptly got up and announced that we had better be going for time was getting on. It seemed to do the trick. Once in the car, he appeared to close his eyes momentarily. I was relieved. I switched on the Light Programme and increased my speed to eighty miles per hour.

After ten minutes, he sat bolt upright again. Clearly, he hadn't really dozed off. 'Heh son! When we get to the city, can you drop me off near to West London. I need visit an old mate at the Scrubs.'

Well, that did it. Swallowing hard, my voice ramped up another cadence. 'Y…Yo…you don't mean, Worm…*the* – *Wormwood Scrubs,* do you?'

'Of course, sunshine. I *do* mean the old treasure. Spent a short spell there as a guest at Her Majesty's pleasure. Better than a bloomin' hotel if I may say so!'

He stared at me with a wicked grin, thoroughly enjoying my discomfort at the bombshell he had just lobbed into my lap. 'Relax young 'un. It was accidental. Pure fate. Well, it was my first and only time anyway. Do you want to hear more?'

I nodded helplessly. One part of me didn't want to know. On the other hand, I must admit I was fascinated, as I had never, since I started driving picked up someone who had been on the wrong side of the law or had been incarcerated at one of Her Majesty's fine institutions.

'After serving in Suez with the Brits and the French in '56, when that Egyptian bloke Nasser nationalised the canal, I was suddenly demobbed. Back in old Blighty, I suddenly found myself homeless after me missus ran off with a neighbour.'

He angled his face as if looking for sympathy. 'I was a sapper – one of the Corps of Royal engineers clearing the battlefield. I learnt everything about explosives, mines, and the like. So, on Civvy Street – with no job and nowhere to live, I had to do a little job.'

I threw a blank glance at him at the revelations, but he urged me to concentrate on the road, as a large coach suddenly swept by in the outer lane with an audible whoosh. I hung onto the steering for dear life as it suddenly wobbled in its wake.

'Do you really want to hear the rest?'

I was hooked.

'Well, with a couple of mates I made in the army, we heard through the grapevine that that a large butcher's factory in South London was unguarded at the weekends. We sussed out that at one end of the offices, they kept all the takings from wholesalers in a safe until they could get to the bank on the Monday. It was a Saturday night. No moon, pitch black. Perfect! I knew from me mate's reccy, that they only had two guard dogs. So, that night, we scaled the wall, snipped the barbed wire, and immediately threw over chunks of prime beef, followed by a couple of juicy meat balls laced with chloroform. Stupid greedy mutts immediately wolfed the lot and keeled over.'

Noticing that I started to open my mouth in horror, he quickly reassured me that the Rottweilers would recover in a couple of hours. 'No permanent harm done.' He added knowingly.

'From my experience, I was able to immobilise the alarm system. It was child's play. But strike me down with a feather, we faced the biggest safe constructed in two-inch best British engineering steel I'd ever clapped eyes on. Luckily, me mate was an expert with the old acetylene torch and made quick mincemeat of the door. But, the blithering idiot, after he cut a big hole through the casing, in his excitement at seeing all those readies like a kid in Aladdin's Cave or summit, he forgot to turn off the gas flame. And would you Adam and Eve it, the whole perishing stash of fivers and tenners went up in holy smoke!'

'What did you do then?'

'What do you think? We legged it like mad. Some three weeks later the old bill got onto us, as one of the goggles we'd stupidly dropped in the panic had prints all over them from me mate who had burnt through the tips of his gloves. In front of the judge, I got four years as my clean record in the army and a good character reference from one from my ex-commanding officers stood me in good stead. With good behaviour I was out in just over two. From that day onwards, I swore on my dear mother's life, I would go straight from then on, regardless, whether I was broke, homeless or whatever.'

Stupefied, I couldn't think of anything to say. I mean what do you say to someone – a complete, stranger who's just thumbed a lift from you having just confessed that he was a former bank robber and had been an inmate at the Scrubs. Okay, so he and his pals did not ultimately benefit in monetary terms as their intended spoils had gone up in smoke. Mind you, that's no consolation to the owners of the factory who had a fortune burnt to cinders.

The end of the M1 came quite soon. Part of me, who at the beginning of the journey thought, quite naturally, the time was going to drag agonisingly slowly for me as a reluctant listener-driver, now felt sad somewhat that it came to an end all too quickly. At the risk of being accused of being a hypocrite, I must secretly confess that my erstwhile companion kept me thoroughly entertained, and he shortened what could have been a long and boring journey.

Soon after Swiss Cottage, I dropped him off at Lords Cricket Ground so that he could make his way to Scrubs Lane. From there he could visit his pal who was incarcerated at Her Majesty's – (for another offence, I was told).

Nine months later, whilst at work, I happened to turn to a report splashed over the front page in the Evening News, that an audacious robbery had taken place at the National Provincial Bank over the Easter Bank holiday in central London. The perpetrators had got in via a betting shop next to the bank and had tunnelled into the bank vault from the shop, by blowing a hole in the adjoining wall having muffled the explosion using a mattress.

Indentikit pictures released by the CID from witnesses who saw three members of the possible gang loitering outside the betting shop on Good Friday were plastered all over the paper. Furthermore, there was a substantial reward in the appeal for information. I stared hard on the police sketches. I looked again. The second picture had an air of something familiar about it. Mousey, cropped short hair. Narrow faced. Caucasian. Nondescript. Unremarkable profile for all intents and purposes. Clean shaven but had the hint of stubble covering his chin. I looked again. Immediately, there was a flashback to a day last summer, nine months ago about a memorable trip along the motorway.

But he was right; I couldn't possibly swear on oath in court that I, just an ordinary member of the public would in all honesty with one hundred per cent certainty recognise him or someone like him with that very ordinary face. Then on impulse, I picked up a pencil from my desk and started to embellish the picture by colouring in a mass of hair that could be construed in a good light as possibly a stubbly beard like I remembered from that encounter nine months before. The figure then looked so much more familiar.

I was in a bit of a dilemma. *And there it was – staring at me – that tempting reward that could have set me up for life.*

Instinctively, like any good law abiding, citizen, I reached over to pick up the phone to dial the number that was published in the paper.

'Which emergency service?'

'Um…per-police please. I – um…er…want to rep…'

'Scotland Yard. Can I help you sir?'…

Then immediately, I dropped the phone back on to the cradle as if it was too hot to handle. The tussle with my conscience lasted precisely two minutes and thirty-three seconds.

'I wonder what sort of day it's going to be?' groaned Angela Hamlyn as she reluctantly crawled out of her warm bed on a cold February morning. 'Work beckons. Need to pay the mortgage!' she muttered aloud, trying to drown her Monday Morning Blues. Pulling back the curtain, she noticed that it had been raining during the night. Her silver sports car glistened in the drive with a thin damp sheen that had just started to evaporate in the early morning sun.

She quickly changed in the bathroom and vigorously brushed her teeth. Bleary eyed, she stared into the mirror over the basin and grinned laconically at the face glaring back at her. A hint of a faint shadow appeared under her large hazel eyes, a leftover she thought to do with the strain of the last two years when readjusting to a new life of being single again after nine years of marriage. Reverting to her maiden name and moving from her beautiful married home with its acres of grounds in leafy Surrey had been stressful to say the least.

Scolding her reflection, she playfully slapped her cheeks on her delicately sculptured face and quickly and expertly applied her make up. The result cheered her up immensely. 'Not too bad for a thirty-three-year-old beauty exec thrown onto the rubbish heap to swell the singleton statistics!' she laughed drily to herself. Jumping on the scales, she noticed a couple of pounds had crept up over Christmas from overindulging at her parents' home in Cheshire. Must spend some more time at the gym!' she vowed, pinching the side of her waist, even though her colleagues complimented her on her still enviable figure. 'Oh! You're amazingly curvaceous my dear girl!' whistled her old married boss, trying his luck.

Angie carefully checked the kitchen diary as she sipped her coffee. 'It's going to be Valentine's in five days, time. Perhaps, a proper celebration is well overdue? She uttered without much conviction. Three weeks ago, her Decree Nisi had come through. She put it aside for later, so that she could study the papers when she felt in the mood.

After eighteen months of self-imposed singledom, she had thrown herself into work like a dervish and resettled in a roomy well designed, flat near the Barbican.

'It's about time that you had a treat and a bit of fun,' nagged her constant and loyal friend Nadia. 'You can't carry on with this convent-like abstinence forever. You'll end up a bitter old maid! Now Angela, my dearest chum. Please listen to me!' Pulling out a scrap paper, Nadia thrust it under her friend's nose. 'Here is a special secret between girls of our age! There's a unique professional agency I want you to ring...'

And so, overriding her initial reticence and repeated protestations, discreet arrangements had eventually been made with an exclusive, high class introduction agency in the West End called Penfolds. She had been booked into an extremely selective (read, "expensive") prestigious hotel called the Duberry near Hyde Park immediately after Valentine's Day. Specific instructions that her "date" would arrive at 10 pm – discreetly to her room once it was dark. Confidentiality and satisfaction assured were the dedicated mission statements of the hotel as well as the agency, who was one of their major clients.

Now as it happened, on the other side of the city, Charles Laidlaw as marketing director of a successful international advertising agency, had done rather well during the previous year, having secured a sizeable contract from a major national advertiser from the fashion industry was hoping to celebrate in one way or the other. Because it was coming up to his landmark fortieth, his co-directors thought that as a one-off, gift, they would present him with a special trip to the West End and spoil him. On the fifteenth of February, he would be treated to a magnificent lunch at Sheridan's, indulge in an Oriental massage and then a leisurely sauna at an exclusive club in Pall Mall in the evening, followed by a surprise night of unrivalled excitement at the Duberry. The birthday package was carefully arranged with an exclusive agency called Sextons Inc who had texted the itinerary with specific instructions to his phone.

'It would be refreshing to get away from Tiffany for a night,' mused Charlie desperately tussling with his conscience. She'd been increasingly clingy and possessive these last couple of years of their relationship. And now was constantly complaining that her modelling opportunities on the catwalk were getting rarer and rarer even though she was not yet twenty-five. To add to his woes, she had been recently applying pressure about the thorny subject of marriage, which he had been avoiding like the veritable plague having been married once before.

The exclusive Sextons group who had agencies in other major cities, such as Paris, Rome and New York etc., had a vast portfolio of wealthy clients on their books. Suitable candidates for escort and partners assignments were chosen not only for their looks, their high intellect and education, their class quality and personality, but primarily for their strict discretion. Actors, fashion models as well as university graduates made ideal "assets", as they were euphemistically called in the trade.

It was on the day after Valentine's when Angela Hamlyn hailed a black cab and arrived at 6.30 in the evening at the hotel and checked herself into room 1131 with a small overnight valise. As Nadia had predicted, the staff were polite and obsequious to the point of underwhelming. There was no blatant curiosity from fellow guests in the lobby that greeted this smartly dressed, extremely attractive brunette when she requested a light supper of a green salad and grilled chicken breast (minus the onions and garlic) together with a bottle of chilled Chablis to be brought up by room service at quarter past seven. Having said that, Angie's choice of a figure hugging, silk dress in muted lilac which accentuated her figure and her teetering two-inch Jimmy Choo's, nonetheless turned several heads as she entered the Duberry. Inwardly grateful for the admiring glances furtively thrown her way, she soon grew in confidence as her initial trepidation dissipated into thin air.

The days around Valentine's you would surmise is particularly a very busy time being a highlight in the social calendar. Introduction and escort agencies inevitably have a field day. Prestigious hotels with select addresses were understandably over swamped with frantic last-minute bookings. Nevertheless, the *"special date"* that had been arranged for Angie, had had his instructions meticulously mapped out by Penfolds. That evening as part of his routine, he scrupulously showered, changed into one of his smart Italian style suits – one of the wardrobe props that he had used a couple of times on a TV commercial. He was surprised to note that he was not required until ten pm. Stifling an exaggerated yawn, he shrugged and thought of the substantial fee that would be due to him. It would be again routine role play for another ageing housewife he thought disingenuously. And so, with plenty of time in front of him, in preparation from a long boring evening ahead he set out on his train journey to central London from his lodgings outside Crawley shortly after eight fifteen.

Meanwhile back at the Duberry, Angie had indulged in a leisurely bath overflowing to the brim with exotic bubbles that contained Aloe Vera, essential oils, Coconut milk and a host of other unpronounceable ingredients reputed to enhance youthful beauty. (Well, that's what it said on the bottle in the bathroom). Completely relaxed as she had never felt for such a long time, indulgently she started to pamper herself. Cosseted in the hotel's mammoth fluffy towels she sipped a generous glass of ice cold, Chablis and experimented with the vast selection of expensive body moisturisers and skin creams tantalisingly displayed besides the bath. At twenty to ten, she sank between the crisp cotton sheets and flopped like lazy starfish in the gigantic King Size bed having abandoned her flimsy nightdress at the foot of the bed. From the bedside table, she briefly turned a few pages of the latest romantic novel from Mills and Boon. However, she soon discarded it in a fit of disinterest. Swiftly, she turned off the bedside lamp next to her and curled up in a foetal position and listened to her enforced breathing in the stillness of the night whilst purposely trying to contain her inevitable excitement. Completely cocooned in the dark, she then turned on her back and waited in nervous anticipation.

As part and parcel of the special birthday surprise for Charlie Laidlaw, his colleagues had tactfully arranged through the agency for a delightful young actress with a bottle of vintage champagne to greet him in his room. Being well organised, the nubile young blonde had arrived quite early at the hotel. At precisely five past nine she had been discreetly installed in room 1311, quite near to the stairwell. To pass the time away, she immediately switched on the television so as not to miss her favourite soap. And in the interim, she helped herself to the copious drinks from the minibar.

It was well past nine by the time Charlie Laidlaw had showered after the sauna and changed into his expensive apres-ski blazer at the club. Feeling at ease with the world at his one night of freedom from the pressures of business and from Tiffany's boring whinges about life being unfair and her increasing excuses to catch up on her beauty sleep in the spare room, he entered the Duberry with a skip in his step. As instructed, he confidently collected his key with a flourish from the receptionist to his room 1311. Signing in, the young girl wished him a pleasant stay. He glanced at the time on his Rolex. His prearranged rendezvous by the agency was for ten past ten as the climax to his evening. It was still only 9.35 on the hotel clock. And so, he made his way to the bar and downed three Champagne cocktails in rapid succession. He wasn't overly concerned at remaining clear headed, for several hours had elapsed since lunchtime when he was presented with a bottle of Bollinger as part of his work treat. Checking the time again on his watch, he suddenly realised that it was almost ten. It was ten agonising minutes away from the prearranged witching hour. A rush of adrenaline coursed through his veins as the anticipation of the exciting things to come made him giddy. And thus, he weaved his way hazily through the lobby. Making straight towards the lift to the first floor, he felt in his blazer pocket for his key. Puzzled that it was not there, he fumbled again and checked all his pockets in turn, including the back pocket of his trousers. 'What on earth have I done with it?' Charlie muttered out aloud, getting increasingly irritated.

He spun around and returned to the bar in a hurry and impatiently asked the barman if he had left his key there. 'It's cream coloured plastic, the size of a credit card,' he explained, going slightly red in the face. The barman shook his head vigorously and said, 'sorry sir,' and went to serve another guest.

Annoyed with himself, he hurried to reception, and feeling a little sheepish, he tried to explain to the night porter who was now on duty that the young girl had given him a card key when he had checked in just forty-five minutes ago. 'Never mind sir,' said the helpful porter. I can get you a duplicate, if you can give me the room number to save looking it up. Luckily sir, it's all modern 3D technology nowadays! The machine can easily print it off.'

With the time furiously ticking away, Charlie's mind went completely blank for a moment. He scratched his head and took another hurried look at the clock. 'Umm…it's 311…something or other. I think. Erm…No. Hang on! It's 11…13 and… Wait a sec!' Getting increasingly agitated and confused, he smacked his forehead in frustration.

The porter waited patiently with a bemused look. Take your time sir. No rush.'

Charlie hesitated or a minute, now wishing that he had spurned that last glass. 'Got it! I'm sure of it,' he exclaimed. Then he spat out the number, '1…131.' He quickly snatched at his watch. It was now getting on for nine minutes past ten. Without further ado, the porter went into the back office, and after a few minutes or so, triumphantly handed over another key.

Clutching the replacement securely in his hand, Charlie made for the stairs so as not to waste any more time. *I'm going to be late!* he grumbled breathlessly. Panic set in. He ran up the stairs two at a time. On reaching the first floor, he stared at the long and seemingly endless corridor with dismay. Facing him was an enormous array of identical mahogany doors. Then immediately to his left, his eyes fell on a door displaying the number 1311. Something about the combination momentarily flashed in his subconscious.

He then tried to insert his card key into the door. Nothing happened. He uttered a curse and he tried again. Again nothing. He took deep breath trying to calm down and to think more clearly. He glanced over his shoulder and then almost ran down the corridor. To his immense relief, he then spied door 1131 to his right. 'This must be it, thank god!' he screamed to himself as his watch reminded him that it was getting on for seventeen minutes past ten. Gratefully, he inserted the card from his sweaty palms, and like magic it clicked with a satisfying clunk and the door opened.

He crept in cautiously into a large, darkened room. It was pitch black save for a dim light hovering over the bathroom mirror, which came on as he entered the bathroom from the short hallway. It's on a movement sensor he thought with relief. He hurriedly undressed, douched himself quickly in the bidet, rubbed a fingertip of toothpaste on to his tongue and splashed on some agreeable cologne he found next to the basin. He quietly closed the bathroom door and tiptoed stealthily into a darkened bedroom which opened out at the end of the hallway, his excitement palpable.

The 8.44 from Crawley had been cancelled due to a signal's failure. An hour later, the young male model managed to get another train which took him to Clapham Junction. It was now quarter to ten. By all accounts it was now getting seriously late. He was in real fix. All passengers had to exit the station to get a replacement bus service which took him and the others to Victoria Station. Anxiety increased by the minute. By the time he got there it was already ten thirty. A black cab would be quicker to his rendezvous at the hotel he thought; but there again, at that time of night with the theatres emptying he could be stuck in traffic. He decided that the underground would be the best option. It was getting on for eleven by the time he had changed lines.

Thoroughly defeated, he decided that he would have to turn back and return home. It was now far too late for his appointment by any stretch of the imagination. Therefore, he'd have to pretend to Penfolds in the morning that the other party did not keep the appointment. As before, he could simply blame it on the client! Depressed and angry with himself and cursing public transport for his ills, reluctantly he started to make his way back to Crawley by the night bus swearing continually under his breath.

However, in room 1311 the young blonde sent by Sexton's by now had started to doze off. The contents of four empty wine glasses next to the bed had taken their toll. The hot bath accompanied by the nondescript music quietly drifting from her phone had contributed to her constant yawning.

It was getting on for half past ten. 'Another stupid rich idiot not turning up!' she moaned as she checked her watch. 'Never mind; I can do with a good night's rest without interruption,' she consoled herself. But then, there was the added worry of not being paid lurking at the back of her mind. 'Anyway, that's not *my* problem,' she argued, whilst she rehearsed in her head what she was going to say to the agency in the morning.

Meanwhile, completely supine and lying quite still in her luxurious bed at the far end of the hallway of room 1131, Angie was just about to change her mind in a sudden panic of guilt thinking that the appointed magic time had passed, when a warm lean body quietly slipped besides her in the dark. Suddenly, tentative fingers crisscrossed under the duvet crept towards her in gentle exploration. Angie gave an audible gasp.

Whereupon, searching limbs from man to woman snaked expectantly across the gigantic expanse of the bed, and then touched. It was like a jolt of electricity that surged immediately between two highly tactile individuals. Charlie took a deep breath. Intoxicated by the exotic perfume that drifted towards him he instinctively drew the wearer achingly towards him. An ecstatic crescendo of unashamed lust instantaneously enveloped the two of them in that moment of unparalleled joy. When pent up forces of unbridled passion suddenly erupted between two like-minded people, it was as though a dam had just burst which romantics often write about but often fail to describe adequately. In those few precious moments, the two of them felt that they had just died and gone to heaven.

After a while, they fell into a relaxed haze-filled sleep like lovers of old, covetously gripping one another as if their very existence to continue to breathe depended on the other. No words were exchanged as it was completely unnecessary. Two hours later, Angie stirred and rolled invitingly towards him. She was insatiable. Charlie could not believe his luck. Every pore in his body was again on fire. The merest touch by this incredibly sensuous woman lying beside him was electric.

At six in the morning whilst it was still dark, Angie gently prised the man's arm from around her body and quietly slid out of bed. She quickly dressed and delicately crept out of the room clutching her overnight bag to her bosom. A cab was waiting for her which quickly and safely took her back home with a quiet satisfied glow on her face.

It was almost seven when Charlie started to wake up. Dawn was just breaking over the rooftops opposite. He stretched expectantly across the bed. There was a hollow dent in the pillow. There was no one there. She had left without a note or any explanation. He was bereft. The bed now seemed cold and empty. Looking disconsolately around him, he picked up a diaphanous negligee that had been discarded at the foot of the bed. Mournfully, he immediately picked it up and smothered it to his face to savour what was left of her perfume hoping to remind him of what had been. Quickly dressing, he scrunched the flimsy garment into his pocket with a desperate longing to see the extremely passionate and erotically-charged owner again.

As soon as he returned to his office the next day, he telephoned Sextons. Full of superlatives, he complimented them on their professional organisation. When he filled in the survey, he awarded his "date" ten out of ten. With the afterglow of the night before still lingering, he immediately booked for an identical assignation at Duberry's for the following week. The secretary announced proudly across the office, 'That young blonde Cheryl must have really impressed this client. He's booked her again! She deserves a bonus.'

It was some days later when Angela Hamblyn still flushed from the after-effects of her night at the Duberry, sat down in her study to reflect on what was happening in her life. Work was going quite well. The French Perfume Corporation which she represented as Beauty Consultant in the UK was increasing their sales month by month. Staring with bored eyes at the pile of correspondence in front of her that were waiting to be dealt with she exclaimed tiresomely, 'Oh to hell with it. These can damn well wait!' But then on second thoughts, she thought that she had better look properly at the papers her lawyers had sent her regarding her divorce, so that they would be ready for the file to be sanctioned and returned to be finalised. What's more, to ensure that there could possibly be no mistake, or the chance of it getting mislaid, the brown manila folder was clearly labelled in large heavy letters,

"Angela Laidlaw v Charles Laidlaw…
Decree Absolute…pending".

THE INTRODUCTION

In January 1912, the first day of the year like every new chapter, swept in with a vengeance. Pristine snow like a fresh blanket had fallen silently in London overnight. It was impenetrable and it came to cover every available inch of the cityscape that hadn't been ravaged by the sharp frost that had hitherto gripped the capital in the last throes of December. From the large sash window of number 3, Eaton Square, Miss Florence Bartholomew looked out expectantly from her elegant drawing room on the first floor. 'That picture postcard of the tranquil scene of winter will soon be spoilt,' she grumbled, as a cumbersome hackney carriage struggled its way across the covered cobbles at the mouth of the mews opposite carving deep muddy ruts in its wake.

Her dull reverie was sharply broken by the sudden clattering of the brass letter box in the front door as the morning post and Saturday newspaper had just been delivered. In deep thought she slowly made her way down the grand sweep of her wide Victorian staircase into the hallway and picked up the post whilst wondering where Agatha the maid was. Then she suddenly remembered that loyal Agatha had left earlier that day to visit her aged mother in Bromley.

Florence sat down at the breakfast table which had been thoughtfully set by Agatha overnight, and slowly opened the post. There was not much of interest to hold her attention – just a few routine household bills. Irritably she pushed them aside as she slowly sipped some freshly prepared orange juice. Picking up her copy of the Times, out of curiosity her eyes strayed over the Notices. What caught her eye at the top corner of the page was an intriguing entry.

> *"Genuine enquiry for a discreet correspondence with an honourable lady from Britain for an authentic friendship. Please reply in strictest confidence to G.H.W.—P.O. Box No...New York. USA."*

Despite her immediate reservations, Florence's curiosity was aroused. Then blushing somewhat, she scolded herself that it was rather undignified – scandalous even to contemplate such an idea at her mature age of thirty-six, and especially being a lady of refinement on the cusp of London Society. As she delicately took a bite of the homemade scones that Agatha had left under a muslin to keep fresh, she turned the page and scoured the Society News. Nonchalantly, she took in the latest gossip about a recent audience by a foreign diplomat with King George V, as well as the nation's preparations for the monarch's forthcoming coronation in June that summer. And then with some alarm, she took a cursory glance at the depressing headlines dominating the front pages which focused on the gathering storm over the Balkans with Prime Minister Asquith urgently addressing parliament over the dangers of a future conflict in Europe.

Miss Florence Bartholomew had been a lady companion to the late Honourable Mrs Felicity Beacham for the last nineteen years following the death of her beloved parents from consumption. She was an only child, and through Father Noel at her church in Knightsbridge had met Mrs Beacham who had offered a comfortable home and the prospects of a vocation, which in her dire circumstances she could hardly turn down. However, it meant complete devotion to her benefactor, not only reading daily to her but also to helping her with her tapestry, art and music classes as well attending to her every whim to the exclusion of all else. As a formal companion, she was expected to accompany Mrs Beacham to all the society events, such as the Royal Garden Party at the palace, the opera at Covent Garden, the Chelsea Flower Show as well as at the opening of each new season at Royal Ascot being central to the arrangement. However memorable the latter were, the most important occasion and the highlight of the social calendar which she had attended, was when she accompanied her mistress on the day of the coronation of the late King Edward VII at Westminster Abbey ten years ago in August 1902 as the Honourable Mrs Beacham happened to be one of the ladies in waiting to Queen Alexandra, the King's consort.

Friends of her age had all got married, and as time flew by, they gradually lost touch until she had no one to turn to. On several occasions, prospective suitors were discarded after it was discovered that they were simply fortune hunters. Then Mrs Beacham suddenly died peacefully in her sleep at the grand age of seventy-nine last summer. Leaving the residue of the lease to Eaton Square to Florence and an annual income of a thousand pounds for life from the Beachamp estate as well as Mrs Beachamp's personal jewellery, Florence seemingly had everything in life except human contact and companionship. Love and the prospect of marriage and children had been sacrificed in exchange for security and predictability. In hindsight, it was one of the saddest regrets of her life. It was times like this, it cruelly struck home that living in a large city like London on your own without friends and family could be extremely lonely and bleak.

Attempting to reassure her, Agatha the loyal maid who had served the household for almost thirty years, kept reminding Miss Florence that despite the passing years that it was never too late to radically change the course of her life if she really wanted to. And what's more, Agatha observed acutely that Florence had maintained her slim figure with the skilful help of fashionable Edwardian corsetry combined with her routine walks through St James Park together with her health-conscious, eating. And consequently, through the added good grace of the Almighty and the kind genetics from her forebears, her ivory pale skin over a heart-shaped face and large emerald-green eyes was flawless. For years, her beautiful, sumptuous ash-blonde hair swept elegantly into a chignon, attracted several admiring male glances whenever she was seen in public, although the aging Mrs Beacham in her eternal vanity thought that the furtive admiration was really directed surreptitiously towards her rather than her young companion.

Several days later, as the thaw in the weather slowly began, so did Florence Bartholomew's reticence similarly begin to defrost. Agatha had accidently left the page of Notices in the Times carelessly lying about in the study after ripping up the newspaper as kindling for the fire. Florence tut-tutted in congenial admonishment at her maid's carelessness, and was about to consign the paper to the bin when her eyes were drawn back to the advertisement from New York…

"Genuine enquiry for correspondence with an honourable lady from…"

In one rash moment, she went to her desk, and quickly and assiduously wrote out a reply:

"Dear Sir,
  Permit me kind sir to respond to your intriguing notice placed in the London Times on…The writer would not be averse to an ethical pen friendship to seek your kind acquaintance…I was born in London of a genteel family and through God's Good Grace I have been fortunate to be independent etc., etc., (though wisely not mentioning her recent legacy).
  I am your faithful servant,
  Miss F.B.
  P.O.Box No…London, Great Britain"

Having sealed the letter, she was then consumed in a moment of panic that it was a grave mistake. She was about to throw it into the blazing fire when she abruptly changed her mind, and so she thrust the letter underneath the carriage clock on the mantelpiece, half hidden from view.

Three days later Agatha, scrupulously tidy as was her habit, happened to pick up the envelope and posted it at the Royal Mail with the other letters containing cheques to pay utilities and provisions. Four weeks later a letter was delivered to Eaton Square with a postmark from New York. It was now too late to reprimand Agatha. But then Florence's face was in a state of shock, and so she cast the letter aside not daring to touch it as if it was contagious or a sin to even consider the idea simply outrageous. However nevertheless, she eventually overcame her curiosity, so that towards the evening in the stillness of her bedroom she nervously ripped open the envelope.

"Dear Madam,

I am in receipt of your gracious reply for a civilised pen friendship to correspond with a person hitherto unknown. It is appreciated that because the Atlantic Ocean separates us, there will have been no realistic opportunity for an orthodox introduction through an honourable third party to mediate. However, if it pleases you, may I have your kind permission to tell you a little about myself…I am…etc…etc… At the same time, if it further pleases you, I look forward with humble anticipation to learn more about you…

I remain your ever obedient servant,
Mr George H. Whitney."

A bemused smile crossed Florence's face. What would the harm in corresponding with this total stranger? If he was a certified pathological lunatic, a murderous criminal, or a predatory married old man, at least there would be three thousand miles separating us for safety she thought cautiously. And so, for the remainder that year, these two complete strangers continued to correspond avidly with one another. Formality was gradually abandoned in favour of, *"Dear Miss Bartholomew"*. And as spring approached and the daylight hours grew longer, so did their writing in content and frequency. Then soon, their increasing correspondence became even more informal and more personal. And by June, as the weather changed, with the mercury reaching seventy degrees, so their terms of endearment blossomed with unashamed familiarity and intensity. It became, *"Dear Miss Florence"*, which then rapidly metamorphosed into, *"My Dearest Florence"*. Equally, *"Dear Mr Whitney"* eventually became, *"Dear George"*.

When the golden glow of autumn took hold and simultaneously the enchanting colours of the fall in America raised its glorious head, their letters took on a closer more intimate tone, their letters took on a closer, more intimate tenure. Their friendship flourished out of all expectations. They exchanged photographs of each other. Florence had decided that she would send George an earlier picture of herself taken ten years ago at a Royal Garden Party in the summer sunshine because she did not want to jeopardise her now treasured friendship with this gentleman whom she had deliberately or unintentionally given the impression that she was much younger than she really was. On receiving this entrancing picture of this beautiful young girl in a breathtaking Edwardian ankle-length silk dress complete with parasol, he thus sent a younger picture of himself. It had been taken in Central Park years ago after he had graduated from college, having just secured an internship with a firm of some well-known attorneys in Wall Street.

At first, Florence felt a pang of guilt for the deception. But she argued that it wasn't exactly dishonest, for she felt that in all truthfulness and reality that they would never meet due to the immense distance between them. Therefore, why break the illusory vision they had of each other. George felt the same. However, despite this, as each day passed it appeared that both parties simply could not wait for the other's reply. As soon as one wrote back, then without wasting a single minute, the other promptly replied in fulsome terms without as much as murmur. Florence wouldn't admit to Agatha that she prayed desperately for each week to simply hurtle by to avoid the tedious and anxious wait for a letter from George. Her everyday waking hours were consumed through lingering nervously like a smitten schoolgirl by the letter box for the morning post.

In December 1911, following Thanksgiving, George had arranged a telephone call to London to finally speak to Florence, whom by now he thought that he knew absolutely *everything* about her. And of course, in the reverse juxta position, this was indeed reciprocal – she about him. After an awkward five minutes of polite but nervous small talk, George proposed marriage to Florence. In clear deep enunciated tones, he said that he was on bended knee in his office in Wall Street, spurred on by his partners who were waiting in excited expectation in the next office. At once, Florence's beautiful gentle English speaking, voice enraptured him, and he was so overwhelmed in his love for this quintessential English Rose whom he had never actually met. And so, how could she refuse this handsome New Yorker, whom she felt she knew everything about him by now.

'My darling Florence, with all my humble being in front of my good business partners as they bear witness, I entreat you, please leave London and join me in New York to start a new life?' pleaded George. 'We will get married in the spring.'

However, as soon as she put the phone down, overcome in a fit of panic she suddenly had a guilty conscience. George had only got a photograph of her from ten years ago. If he discovered that she had dishonestly concealed her true age, there would be indescribable ramifications, not least considerable consequences from her blatant deception. Although realistically, despite the age deception, she was still incomparably beautiful at thirty-seven, even though small laughter lines had inevitably crept around the eyes and jawline in an otherwise unmarked face. And then there was the small matter of a little thickening around the waist which her bodice was recently having some difficulty in containing.

And so, after considerable soul searching and a torrent of tears, she decided to call off the betrothal. Solicitously, Agatha offered that she was a fool to miss this opportunity of a lifetime to marry this American gentleman lawyer who was genuinely devoted to her. And so, with a heavy heart, Florence wrote a letter to explain why the engagement must be broken off and that the wedding could not possibly take place. 'You must choose a younger bride who would be more compatible with your age.' She suggested generously. In the letter she had enclosed a more recent photograph of herself – head and shoulders – passport size and taken more in the cold realistic light of autumn.

Immediately on receipt of this letter, George arranged another call to Florence and begged her to reconsider his proposal, and furthermore admitted that he too had a confession to make. He said that he had also sent a younger photograph of himself to impress Florence, because he thought that she would not entertain the idea of her marrying someone much older.

Swallowing hard, he conceded that he in fact was nearing forty, and that his temples were greying somewhat even though luckily, he still had a full head of hair. And what is more, that through overindulging in the ubiquitous business lunch, he had inevitably put on a few pounds around the middle! But despite everything, he declared unequivocally that he truly loved only her, and that she was even more delectable now at her age, and furthermore, that he was determined to marry her whatever the circumstances so that they could share their destiny and future lives together.

And so, overcome with her happiness now complete, Miss Florence Bartholomew was now able to look forward to a joyful future with a new life in the New World. On the 10th April 1912, accompanied by her loyal maid Agatha Barker as chaperone and companion, they took a train – first class to Southampton docks. With a sizeable trunk full of her bridal trousseau from Harrods and all her worldly possessions, Florence together with over two thousand passengers (amidst the raucous fanfare from good wishers scattered amongst the mass of sightseers at the quayside) immediately prepared to embark on the newly commissioned, gigantic ocean liner called, *RMS Titanic* on its maiden voyage to New York. Heady with excitement, Florence and Agatha made their way to their luxurious cabin on the upper deck. Shortly after 1.30 pm that day, this formidable state-of-the art, passenger steam ship set sail. It was anticipated that, seven days from hence onwards – on the 17th April, waiting impatiently at the dockside on Pier No 54 in New York Harbour would be the steadfast Mr George Henry Whitney who would be anxiously waiting to greet his long-awaited bride to be…

Whereupon, after collecting further passengers and supplies at Cherbourg, France and then Queenstown, Ireland, this gigantic luxury liner started to cross the Atlantic at full tilt on its memorable journey. By the early hours of the 15th April 1912 – 12.40 am to be precise – just off the coast of Newfoundland in mid Atlantic…something momentous was about to happen*…

*Epilogue:
After striking a gigantic iceberg off the coast of Newfoundland, out of 2240 passengers and crew, more than 1500 lost their lives when the

Titanic capsized and sank. It would take another seventy-three long years for divers to discover the wreck of the Titanic lying 13,000 feet in its watery grave at the bottom of the ocean.

Remarkably after this passage of several decades, a considerable tranche of relics from the ocean liner had now been recently found on the seabed that had not completely disintegrated through natural decay, or from being destroyed by marine creatures, or by the erosion from salt water, rust and even metal and wood-eating bacteria. Despite this, recent deep sea, images had managed to photograph leather shoes scattered amongst the debris. However, when historians look back, they and we would never really know whether the shoes once belonging to the tragic Miss Bartholomew (or in fact, any other of her personal effects) had ultimately likewise been found, and whereupon identified with absolute certainty that they once belonged to this particular lady.

And furthermore, because some of the passenger records at that time, were often confusing or at best incomplete, perhaps the enduring answer of the actual fate of Miss Florence Bartholomew would remain a mystery for eternity amongst these historical artifacts that had managed to survive the destructive ravages of time.

And what happened you may reasonably ask, to the loyal and forever-patient Mr George H. Whitney? It was said that two years later in 1914 at the start of the First World War, it was reported that he drowned whilst swimming in the sea after spending each morning searching in vain across the ocean for sight of his beloved Florence. Others said that he died of a broken heart and willingly went to join his true and only love in her watery grave.

...and thus however, this story would now be sadly and tragically consigned to the annals of history – for ever after...

THE DRAGONFLY KITE

Excerpt from The Ancestral Quest by F.L.Ying (Aka F.G.Kwong)

"Love, Grief and Hope through the Conflict of War and across the Racial Divide. A Family's Journey of Survival from Ancient China to the West. A True Story torn between Two Worlds."

(In 1946, after the devastating bombing in the Blitz on Liverpool in the war, Kwong Chun Ji fled with his family and sought refuge in Wrexham, North Wales to start again. He started again in a laundry, trying to get on with his Welsh neighbours in Pen-y-Bryn). Francis, the eldest son takes up the story...

By the spring of 1949, Uncle Chun Tileng had recovered sufficiently from TB to be brought home from the sanatorium from the Minera Mountains. As he gradually regained his strength, he threw himself into work like a dervish as though to make up for lost time, and also to repay his debt to my father – his older brother. After work, they reminisced about their ancestral home in China, and little by little got to know one another. (As Chun Ji had already left China for the West in 1921 by the time Chun Tileng was born). When time allowed, they would take it turns to practice the *Zhu* – an ancient string instrument, rather like a zither – Uncle had brought from China, which used to belong to their late father. By striking the wired strings (which were strung over the belly of the hollow rectangular body made of polished rosewood) with a pair of bamboo flails, one could produce a high-pitched sound from its short range. The alien sound which sounded like a strangled top C to a non-oriental ear, unfortunately made Nero, the family's pet black cat bolt out of the house in terror – never to return. Such musical evenings reminded the brothers of old China, when families had time to play and sing together after a hard day's toil in the fields around their home in Taishan.

From time to time, a pastor from the Chinese Church based in Liverpool would visit to help the children learn Chinese. Uncle continued the lessons in his absence using simple texts from the religious books the pastor would leave. My father not having been brought up in the Christian faith, found it conflicted with the beliefs of Buddhism and ancestral worship in which he had been raised – although now lapsed. Therefore, with extreme difficulty, he tried to come to terms with the fact that his children were leaning towards Western religious beliefs, especially when the four oldest started to attend the local Sunday school in the centre of town. This conflict was compounded by the fact that earlier he had agreed for all his children to be christened in the Church of England.

'At least the children are still being immersed in the Chinese language regardless of the contents of the texts,' said Uncle to pacify him.

However, Father was still determined to prevent the family from being radically changed by the Western way of life. But day by day, an irreversible wedge was driven into his futile attempts to keep his children imbued in the ways of ancient Chinese culture. It was an impossible task thought Uncle, bearing in mind that the children had been born and bred in Britain. But he did not dare to offer his opinion to his older brother, especially one who was also head of the family clan.

Although the immediate neighbours in Pen-y-Bryn were perfectly at ease with having a Chinese family in their midst, there were rumblings within the wider community around Wrexham who feared that a floodgate would be opened if too many foreign migrants came to settle in the locality. At present, the total Chinese population consisted of no more than six families in the whole of the area. Irrational though it may seem, fears of the unfamiliar – particularly with regards to foreigners who did not speak the language, and physically stuck out like sore thumb and who had different customs – inevitably caused some disquiet in certain pockets of the community. Resentment and ignorant gossip about "an invasion of foreigners" had already started to fester because of the establishment of the Polish Hospital in Maelor nearby, which led to a rapid increase in the number of Polish families settling in the area after the war.

Now as it happened, by midsummer, a kite competition was scheduled to take place at the Wrexham Recreation Park across the road from Pen-y-Bryn. The organisers had retrieved some wreckage of a German warplane which had been brought down during the air raids over Merseyside, and the local community planned to have a bonfire with it together with a firework display and kite flying.

Not surprisingly, that day stuck indelibly in my mind. Although I was somewhat afraid of my father's reaction to my speaking to him without his specific permission, I decided to tell him that my school friend Colin had told me about the kite competition. Father just grunted, as if to ignore me. But to our surprise and secret delight, my brother and sisters noticed that in the evenings at the end of the working day, he and Uncle started to put together a Chinese kite. Shaped like a gigantic dragonfly, its wingspan was at least four feet with a long tapering body and tail. The skeleton was made from thin strips of bamboo cane which Father had bent into shape by soaking it in water. Using twine, the bamboo was skilfully bound into a three-dimensional shape whilst still submerged. After seven days, the twine was removed and the whole left to dry in the open air. Stretched over the frame, he glued stiff greaseproof paper which had been soaked in turpentine and then coated in varnish.

Enormous black and red dragon eyes were painted on the head with two thin wires protruding as antennae. We noticed that he had secured a roll of string which measured over one hundred feet to pinpoint attachments on the kite; one on the underside of each wing and one under the belly of the body.

The day came for its inaugural flight, which would either be a real test of my father's ingenuity or end with him red-faced in embarrassment. I told Colin to bring his family, including his older brother Arthur who had just returned from serving in the forces in Aden. It was the last day in July. A hot and balmy evening welcomed the local population. They arrived in their hundreds with their children and pet dogs in tow. Fathers clutched their precious kites

– all homemade, and everyone was desperate to show off their skills and workmanship. By 9 pm, the bonfire was roaring away in the sultry summer's evening. It was a clear black night with a carpet of stars so sharply in evidence that it was if they had been painted in silver on a giant canvas. The organisers welcomed everyone to the sound of fireworks exploding in the night sky. Luckily, a sharp breeze was whipping up as the competitors unfurled and launched their beautifully painted kites into the air. Most of them were traditional diamond shape. Some were box shaped and flew haphazardly around the park, some reaching fifty feet or more.

I remember the strange look of hostility received from the locals as Father placed his kite on the grass verge next to the roaring bonfire; though our neighbours – particularly Mr Gareth Young from the drycleaning shop across the road and Mr Willy Jones, the baker who had lent Father his industrial bread oven to cook our large turkey last Christmas – gave us a smile of encouragement.

'That foreign monstrosity won't even get off the ground!' snorted an extremely large, rotund man wearing a string vest that was a bit small for him. Derisively, he poked the tail of Father's kite with his foot as soon as he and Uncle started to unpack the rest of it.

'Wrong shape! Too ugly! And too blinkin' heavy!' catcalled another man, whose tiny kite had just fluttered limply and crashed to the ground after a lull in the breeze.

Hundreds of heads turned to stare at us. Disapproving silence greeted Father and Uncle, who did not say anything, but took deliberate and measured steps away from each other. Uncle carried the belly of the Chinese kite across his body and Father simultaneously began to unravel the coil of string.

Just then, the cooperative breeze that had been blowing all evening suddenly stopped dead in its tracks. My brother and sisters and I crossed our fingers and said a silent prayer for a hurricane to whip up and save our family's face.

'I'd pack up if I were you mate!' sneered another onlooker to guffaws of support from his pals.

No sooner had those words been uttered than the breeze picked up. Encouragingly, Father felt a sharp tug as the faint breeze gave some lift from under the belly of the kite. Keeping the line taut, Father nodded a signal to Uncle to throw the Dragonfly Kite face into the wind, which thankfully was now increasing to a welcoming swell. At ten feet parallel to the ground, the kite started to fly. The crowd held its breath.

But suddenly, our hearts sank as the kite began to struggle. It appeared to be nosediving into the ground, straight into the dying embers of the bonfire. Then all at once, the wind whipped up as if a storm was in the offing. Father quickly fed out the string and the kite at once started to soar, giving a noisy flap of its wings as the wind propelled it upwards as though it were heading for the stars. Higher and yet higher it went as the string was fed out to its maximum. The locals had never seen anything like it before.

Oohs and aahs greeted the spectacle as the kite dipped and zigzagged majestically in the summer night sky, illuminated by the stars in the background and the glow from the bonfire below which had found new lease of life due to the fresh blast of wind.

Later, Mother told me that Father hadn't flown a kite since he was a boy of thirteen at the ceremony of the cutting off, of the much-hated pigtails, when his village back in China celebrated the end of the Ch'ing Dynasty in 1912 with the fall of the last emperor.

After twenty minutes or so, Father and Uncle brought the kite down to the ground. They were immediately surrounded by scores of locals, who clapped spontaneously at the display.

'*Well done!*' shouted Mr Young from the drycleaning shop.

'*That was brilliant, Mr Kwong!*' said Willy Jones, the baker.

At once many kite fliers gathered around to examine Father's kite. They wanted to know how to build one like it. Father then explained in his broken English and with much gesticulation how it had been built.

'It is to do with the bowed shape of the wings being buoyed by the air like in an aeroplane. The weight of the kite is supported in the air as air streams move above and below the wings giving it a sandwich effect which buffets it,' he said, quite matter-of-factly.

The success of the Chinese kite, which had reached record heights never achieved previously by any other kite in Wrexham, had won the cynics over. My friend Colin said that most of the locals would never look at our Chinese family in the same suspicious manner again. At that moment, I felt a sudden burst of pride in being Chinese and ethnically different, when hitherto I had often craved to be like one of the indigenous locals so that I could melt anonymously into the background.

After the display, Father, Uncle and my sisters left promptly to return home. Colin, my brother Alan and I, together with another boy called Johnny Lewis who knew Colin, dragged our feet because we wanted to see the end of the fireworks. When we left the park via the exit at the end of Pen-y-Bryn, which was besides the side entrance of the local garage, we were in high spirits and did not want the night to end. Colin and Johnny Lewis gave us some fireworks they had produced out of their pockets and cock-a-hoop, we lit them and threw them into the air. Unfortunately, one of the fireworks, known as a Volcanic Banger, ended up over the wall of the garage yard and landed in a pile of old rubber tyres.

Within minutes they caught fire. A tiny spark rapidly became a raging fire. As the rancid black smoke plumed into the air we were stunned at the ferocity of the blaze. Naturally frightened we all ran home as fast as our legs could carry us.

Then remarkably quickly, two fire engines rushed up the hill from the town centre and got the blaze under control. Scared out of our wits, my brother and I hid under our blankets in our bunk beds not daring to tell our parents what had happened.

Shortly after midnight, a policeman and a member of the fire crew knocked on our parents' shop door. Shame faced, we were dragged out of bed by my irate father who yelled at me because I was the older brother, and he blamed me for leading young Alan astray and for bringing shame on the family. My father threatened to punish me, and punish me he did, with three stokes of the willow across my backside. The police officer said that was enough punishment and added to my father, that by the way, everyone enjoyed his amazing kite display.

The following morning, Father went to see the garage owner and offered to pay for the damage. To his surprise, the owner said that he wasn't overly worried as only old, worn tyres had been destroyed, and that fortunately the blaze hadn't spread to the petrol pumps. He said that he had wanted to dispose of the tyres for months as they were blocking up his yard! What is more, he said that he would make a claim for the loss of new tyres from the insurance. To make amends, Father did not charge him for his laundry for many weeks. I was put on gruel and plain rice, soaked in dripping. I accepted the punishment like a man, for I didn't want to reveal the name of the boy who had thrown the offending firework that had almost burnt down the local garage. It seemed at the age of nine, I preferred to be called a Chinese pyromaniac rather be labelled a treacherous snitch!

"A DANGEROUS RIDDLE OF CHANCE"
by F L Ying

"Murder, mystery and mayhem in a battle of against the evil Custodians of Terror from an Alterworld."

When an unusual group of friends embark on an adventure, they face dangerous challenges beyond their imagining. Chance, a cheerful harlequin of goodness and kindness and his sidekick Henry de Poisson must solve a riddle to extend his life on earth, so that he can unite the Three Kingdoms (One of flora, one of animals and that of humans) and save the planet from destruction.

Confronting Chance and his young friends – Tim Needles, who's ten, Lotte Pert, aged thirteen, and their dog, Ram at a circus at World's End, is his evil nemesis, the sinister Dr Slatane De'Aff who has sent by the mysterious Qnevilus from the Alterworld to kill Chance and all do-gooders who stand in their way.

Chance, who magically came to life from a wooden statue has only ninety-nine days on earth to carry out his mission as predicted by Cecil-the-Thin, a ghostly soothsayer before he implodes in a puff of smoke. Can the precious Gem of Knowledge in his possession save him and his friends from certain death? Will good triumph over evil?

.

THE MUSE OF YESTERYEAR

As if embarrassed she lowered her eyes rapidly which were now welling up. Her breath now in short sharp gasps. 'I can't give you any more of myself than I have these last couple of years,' she wailed, for her awful anguish was now palpable. Distraught, she suddenly realised that it was the final chapter of their last story together. 'I cannot give you anything more than this vital piece of my work!' she said through falling tears, thrusting a crumpled file of papers into his hands.

In disbelief, he stared at her not daring to admit to himself what was really happening. The chilly air around their shoulders hung like a fog suspended in mid-air as the temperature outside their building began to plummet. Squaring up to him, she hissed between gritted teeth, 'You belong to another, and about to be tied! Whereas I am now free – completely free to...' The inflection in her voice petered out several decibels as though in intractable pain.

'What? You mean *free* as a common butterfly...to flit from one to another,' he retorted jealously, for which he had no reasonable right to do so, given the situation. 'You can't suddenly just get up and go and leave me. I can't possibly continue to write without your help!' He spread his hands in a helpless gesture, trying to stop her leaving.

Pulling on her coat, she spun on her heels towards the door of their flat. Over her shoulders she said, 'look. I've scribbled down much of what was in my thoughts from these last two summers of meeting you. Do what you want with them. My work is precious; it's like my only child!' Publish if you dare. Consider that it's my last gift to you for old time's sake. It's a window into my mind – perhaps partly into my heart, but *never* from my soul!' she added covetously.

The door slammed shut with a bang of finality and rattled the windows in their frames. Completely stunned, he shook his head to stir into action, and like a madman rushed into the street to look for her. She was nowhere to be seen. She had vanished like magic into the bowels of the city ether.

And so, for thirty odd years he searched high and low for his former love and muse in every corner of the country without success. Enquiries through newspaper notices also drew a dead blank, despite the name of Juliet Smith being incredibly common.

'On reflection, she would be an old woman by now,' he murmured sadly as his ancient knees creaked towards his desk. Although thinking about it, he was now old as well. 'I'll dedicate the legacy of her work in her name,' he muttered generously. 'To make amends for what happened to us all those years ago. I know I'll call it,' *"A Window into her Heart and a Revelation into her Soul."* 'It would be a lasting epitaph to her. I hope it's not too late,' he added as an afterthought as he religiously scrutinised the weekly Obituary Notices.

JULIET SMITH – IN SEARCH OF A MUSE ONCE LOST

If I could command a dictionary of words,
It would save a myriad amount of melodrama.
Was it for the simple sake of writing about it?
Or was it just for your sake or was it purely for mine?
I know I have said it all before:
Each line no different from the rest,
One this week: again, one the last.
Each sentence the structure of which more difficult to digest.
Then it's the same this year you've raised the bar,
And no different to that from a year ago
When the gauntlet thrown down pulled us apart.

But ah, you have forgotten one empirical thing.
When I write one word you write two…
But never the same or in the same breath:
I say them not for want of boasting or an attempt to carp.
I repeat them again to avoid a threat.
You pause for a thought which is like death.
Therefore, no tantrum fits to impress a king,
No reason or plot to alter a thing.

After all it's two ordinary people in a joust of thirst:
To compete in the race of who thought of it first,
To reveal one's hand so soon the game could be lost.
The end is in view long before it began.
I write down a line of virgin verse –
You cancel it out in one quick burst,
Of didactic prose which is a noble choice,
Then of rhyming couplets you find a voice.
And what else are you thinking, will it justify despair?
But do you think as I do, praise beauty and wonder?

I'm accused of spoilt stanzas that still fly through the air.
Pure words are like art and rare music to ponder
This nectar of life can embellish our cares.
But there again, sometimes you use sly limerick slang,
Which caused our egos collide with an almighty bang.

So please put away those mocking wit eyes.
It's better to talk to yourself than write at a suicidal pace,
When composing an essay on what's right or what is wrong.
Yet I can see in your writing which is etched on your face,
Expressions suppressed will come eventually to light.
Those prosaic kind phrases with emotions disguised,
When baring your soul often hiding a fight.
The Bard may forgive and permit borrowing this time,
A plea for a muse once lost in that immortal line…
"Juliet. Oh Juliet. Where art thou Juliet?"

CHAPTER II

© Juliet Smith

The muse that vanished off the face of the earth.

Mystery of the Missing Poetess, circa 1970

(Will the real Juliet Smith get in contact)

Love Poems for an Unknown Stranger

UNREQUITED

Her love was not as his was,
For neither was it pure.
She gave her all, 'til he could want no more.
He seemed to use her.
Did she use him?
His love like a dancing sunbeam,
Scarred her brain; that teeming brain.
Her love though patient, wasn't that understanding.
It did not win him over.
Worthless – yet still lacking.
It lacked that certain spark to give her life of joy,
With auras of brilliant splendour.
She could but strive,
And strive for completeness with another one.
For arms half-stretched out are not enough,
As true effort of love has to be supreme.

ATTRACTION UNFOUNDED

He to her and her to him
But 'twas in all a passing whim.
She was free, free to care,
To care he did not really dare.
Perhaps indulge in passing interest
To fate was left the unknown rest.

He was tied, love nearly complete,
Whilst she was still had her love to seek.
Thus, danger lurked behind success,
And yet his soul was full of restlessness.
Conquer her, he wished he could,
Yet its another matter if he would!

'Twas all for nought they both really knew,
That attraction dies as humans do,
For her to seek once more in vain.
Or perhaps true love yet to sustain,
Whilst he content, with what he had,
For he had never intended to be bad!

HOPE

Hope like a setting sun,
it sinks so slowly.
The time is indefinable,
for clouds gather one after another
Like hands stretching lazily
to cover that ball of gold.
But gloomy thoughts gather,
'til only a ray is left,
For me they never seem to disappear,
and never to fade.
However thin and slight –
redeeming and soon to wipe away,
Those heavy leaden skies of gloom
that starts growing once more,
Until a bright new hope returns again.

A SEARCH FOR PEACE

Oh, for peace of mind,
and end to restlessness,
But where can these I find?

Indecision sets in
like wormwood – ruthless.
But will I ever win?

A brain with no peace,
disquiet with worries.
Is there no release?

The search I continue still,
but am I to remain searching,
To seek my whole life through.

INFLUENCES

Influences from those you love,
And from those you don't.
Which are you, to take as true?
Which to reject outright from you?
Life is one long anxious choice,
A choosing without an end.
What if you choose wrongly?
With mistakes your whole life long.

If only you could start without
A pressure from somewhere around you,
Then conscience clear as dawn anew.
Your own standards could then be drawn.
But without influences good or bad,
What would your life then turn out to be?
A shadow lost, a dream unformed,
A life that's empty and gone un-mourned.
Or perhaps there is a shining way,
Of life as it should be lived today

COMFORT

What is this thing called comfort?
Where does it come from?
Who can give it?
And from where?
To ease the soul
And right the wrong.

Those closest are far away.
What of friends,
They do not know.
Should you stoop to plead?

Nought's to be done,
But look ahead,
And be your happy self.
Self-pity must be overcome,
Although your heart is of lead.

PETUNIAS

The petunias blossom
By the old stone wall,
Blue with age,
They glow unwanted.
And so insecure,
Their glory passes
As ours are quickly over now,
Cast deep in a shadow.
But not always is it when
Perchance a child will pass,
And see their longing to look.
Then they reach out to pick,
For they'll scream out in pain.
The sacrifice of love growing,
To die alone without a gain.

ONCE MORE

She stood alone once more,
White crystals frost fell in abundance.
Fell they did upon her heart,
She had been warm at the start.
But now what happens?
She saw nothing there,
As her tears turned
To drops of white of ice
The light she spurned.

All warmth ended as she stood alone.
A shape evolved from the frost and ice.
Was it he now returning
To her to save or cast her off?
But how could she know.
So, she sank to her knees
Under his grey shadow looming, which
Dropped away as ice turned to snow.

CAT

She sits over there,
Curled up in her chair.
How could she know?
How much I care.
I tickle her chin
With an affectionate grin,
For she and I know
That he'll soon be in.

With his eyes aglow
He enters; we purr,
For he likes her too
As we both sit and stir.
The green eyes clear
From her cheeks like tears.
And as he approaches,
She stares and then peers.

Then there we all are
In front of the fire
Our troubles quite gone,
For our minds are at one
We gaze at her there,
Between us a pair,
With peace in her eyes
As they glitter and stare.

A fathomless green,
Those eyes to be seen,
For those who dare look,
They're clear as fresh stream.

Why can't our lives,
Be like a cat's third eyes?
Large, shining, and rare
At rest and so relaxed.

But for now; not too long
For peace will soon gone,
As her eyes gently close
Dare not disturb her in repose.
And so, we'll creep away,
Both, on the tips of our toes.
Will we ever find such peace?
Elsewhere, but it's always exposed.

THE STUDENT

He started so high
above the clouds.
There to stay,
perhaps for a day,
To get there again
in years to come.

The clouds become grey,
heavy and inert.
They bored him so -
so down he had to go!
Down and yet down,
dragged by the weeds.

The weeds of wrong,
the seeds of discontent.
It pulled him down,
but was he to drown?
Or would the future
restore him as before?

As yet he knew not,
nor really cared,
But he wallowed with
those choking weeds,
Growing higher around him.

One day he noticed
the clean white clouds.
The blueness of the clear blue sky,
his weeds began at last to die.
Hope returned, bounding, and
leaping above the clouds so high.

GONE

He walked away
and left her there,
Alone and bare,
his mind was gone.
But hers was at rest,
as he left her there
At his behest.

The sun was stark,
as it beat down,
Upon her body,
golden brown.
She lay stiff and cold,
in pools of red
That ran all around.

Unknown to her,
he came in vain.
Shock and pain,
that went and came.
It was over in sunbeam blink,
But the sand was wet.

He never knew her,
but she knew of him.
For he then ended,
what was to him…
In foolish doubt, just then,
For both transient lives
with a dubious sadness end.

UNKNOWN

What can this be that haunts her so,
That's always there
To make her care.
Love is unknown and so is this.
What can be done to make her one
With her fellow men?
And those who care,
But dare not dare for
They know not what.

Is it anger, lust or shame?
That makes her so
That she cannot gain.
What is needed above all
That strange unknown,
The world of love,
And understanding.
More should be there,
But how many of those
Does she believe that really care?

One day a light will shine so bright,
Then she will know
What is pure and right…
Then no more worries, strain, or stress
Will cloud those eyes of trouble.
And in their place
Will come a look,
Of contentment and of peace
To brighten all our lives.

DIVORCE

Which was it to be?
She knew not how, but cared
So much, as not to see,
Whether it should be you or me.
Both ways she was destined drawn
Which of us would ultimately win,
And which of us left to mourn.

She felt alone and torn
With grief and uncertainty.
And wished that she could retain
The age of immaturity
When all was simple and easy.

We knew not the best,
She knows not either yet.
As eyes grow damp…
The time will have to be met,
And until that misty eve
We wait and hope and sigh,
And wonder why.

It had to happen as it did.
It will fall, that strange event
Then we will know
To which she'll claw and cleave.
And which of us she will eventually leave.

DISAPPOINTMENT

It was a barmy evening,
As I patiently waited.
The sunset was classical,
And as I squinted at it,
With hooded eyes,
My hope of what was to come
Was forever unending….
Night came creeping down the hill.

Was I to be disappointed,
After so much waiting?
But surely not, for it was getting late.
Then gradually I knew,
That I was out of luck,
For no one came.
When I, the flea shook with might
For not a human did I bite!

FOOLISH ATTRACTION

He thought that he could win her at forty odd!
She thought the proposal an exciting sin
In her innocent state of youthfulness.
For he had money, charm and a car,
Though she towered over him, his five-foot five.
Thinking going out with him could do no harm,
But conceit anew led him to woo.
She brushed him off, sounding the alarm,
Gently at first, but then more firmly
As light attracts a moth fluttering. Though
This just increased his thirst unquenched.

As a friend of those, she loved the best.
She could do nought but else,
Her truth and honour put to the test.
But her love complete could not be bought,
For all he offered impressed her not.
And ultimately, that's all he got,
Was a thwarted heart to tend and mend.
Her love and will she'd give not easily,
For his could never sadly be in the end.

A TRANSIENT HAPPINESS

Happiness was for the moment.
It came and soon was spent.
That thing elusive that we all hunt after,
Which I was chasing blindly
After him – his love and laughter.

But he, did he really want only me?
I could but hope he'd eventually see
Where my happiness exposed as hunger,
Ready to give yet even faster,
So obvious was my longing.

Did he truly love her still?
Was he ruled by her iron will?
Or fear of what she would do.
Would I ever hope to win?
Or bid goodbye, so sad adieu.

So, in confusion I naively stay
A stubborn fool,
His words that past,
A heavy weight that lasts.
To leave her all alone for me I crave,
Is this the happiness I'd want to save?

LIGHT

He had to look forward,
Never to look back.
What lay before,
What did it lack?
Darkness was behind his,
Yet it lingered on.
And he seemed to be,
Surrounded by depth,
Height and width.

No one can bring
That horizon forward
While his dull
Carelessness and pain
Increased until
That day a light came.
It came from nowhere,
But filled his being,
'Til he found time to care
For what lay ahead,
And gone was his dread.
The light settled around him,
Brilliant and rare.

THE END

She saw it happen,
One cold bright day.
The clinging dew still grey
And flowers closed their petals,
For a tree dies as so they may.

But this was different,
Of this she knew,
But why, she had no clue.
She watched it happen,
Slowly wither and die all way through.

The buttercups scattered around,
Painted faces upward turned.
They all mourned quietly,
Even the drops of dew.
Perhaps, they the answer knew?

Not only did its body die,
But its great proud soul cut adrift.
In the sky a bell did toll.
It had crossed the river wide,
As birds would roll in its fateful dust.

She stood filled with shock and awe,
To see the silvered dust once more.
Can pride of life now rest in peace?
For then she knew, like this tree nearby
Was humbled now to nothingness.

CHAPTER III

© Simon Holder

Television Director. Broadcaster. Scriptwriter. Lives in Wiltshire. Poet. Author of:

The Revolution of The Species.
A topical and terrifying environmental thriller

For The Love of a Life.
An unusual international love story

It's All in The Script.
A dastardly, humorous thriller involving a present-day TV soap opera set in the 18th Century

A Cultured Pearl and other Tales.
Of love, longing, mystique, and hope

(King Lear Short Stories Awards. Commendation for A Cultured Pearl. 2023)

Satirical Reflections

Rhymes for Our Times

PIERCINGS

On each of our bodies we have eight or so holes
For various reasons to aerate our souls.
Or for sight, or for hearing, breathing and poo,
And all quite enough for what we must do.
In the kitchen a colander does much the same job,
Like draining hot water from corn on the cob.
So why is it now that so many want more,
Drilling through skin as if in a war;
Nose-drops, earrings, bolts, pendants and gonks,
Through tongues, lips, stomachs, brows and conks.
Septicaemia's rife when one has these strange things,
But it's said to be *cool* to have these piercings!

Without some you're old, not part of the clan,
Yet I'd rather be that and complete as a man!
And when I've a cold, and am blowing my nose,
Know the snot is contained and won't cover my clothes
By flying out my breather in many directions
And distributing it all over some lady's collections!
A vicar is holy, but not full of holes –
So why tunnel our skin like burrowing moles?
Girls have them, too, often piercing each breast
With dumbbells, rings, diamonds and all the rest!
And better less said about what's pierced below-
It would make me blush to reveal what I know!
So why do we do it, this adding of "bits?"
Oh, save us from piercings, they're really the pits!

SCRUFFINESS

When I travel around, on foot, bus or train,
People's looks vex me: please let me explain.
For despite sanitation, loos, showers on tap,
Why is unkemptness the new modern rap?
Even those in top jobs seem to have just left their bed,
With tousled hair, unshaven – and eyelids still red.
Their clothes ill-fitting – un-ironed with multiple creases,
And all un-matching, like from differing pieces;
Odd socks, no ties, frayed shirts and slashes,
Like they'd been in a fight or several car crashes.
Unclean scuffed shoes or broken trainers,
Is it a way of expression for our race of complainers?
Is life such a chore, or perhaps just too tough?
That we have to go round as an unchallenged scruff.
Is it laziness? Fashion? That now strangely disdains
The sanitation of progress achieved by our brains.

Formerly even the needy, far too poor to ablute
At least had some pride and went round in a suit!
I won't leave without shaving (unless my flat's on fire)
Because I cannot abide any scruffy attire.
But now often I'm stared at, for being a tad formal,
A throwback to ages when smart was quite normal.
It is just laziness, when we've got showers, bidets, baths,
Not to cleanse our bodies of our lives, aftermath.
So, despite better hygiene, few now look their best,
Preferring holed and soiled jeans with a stained, torrid vest:
A moth-eaten jersey on un-ironed, torn shirt,
Its provenance featured by stains, muck and dirt!
For being well groomed or "smart" now brands one fool
And looking scruffily dirty is the ultimate "cool!"

MOBILES

There's nothing worse than a mobile call that's only halfway heard,
As one strains on the train to imagine
The other's missing phrase or word.
Passengers listen intensely wrapt from behind their papers curled,
Secretly imagining backgrounds to that steamy, unknown world.
Sex, scandal, intrigue, murder …
Mistress, lover, new-leaked government files
Help the journey as the train speeds on, fast eating up the miles.
And then into the torrid tale another mobile rings –
Confusion reigns supreme …
Blotting out what's happening in the first licentious scene!

And so, the tempted ears extend
Into *both* the sizzling stories' crannies,
Tuning in to macho man, new bride
Or trembling, awe-struck grannies.
But with both calls at different points of such disparate narrations,
The interest wanes, as the train speeds on
Through life's turgid, fleeting stations.
So the threads are lost –
And resigned annoyance casts a disappointed pall,
Because really one just wished the phones had never rung at all!

COMPUTERS

What would we do without these machines,
Which govern our lives, our money, our dreams?
Waste our time with loved ones? Read a brilliant book?
Or prepare a lovely meal, which takes two hours to cook?
Or a country walk, a drink in a pub,
A theatre or a smash hit film and then some tasty grub?
Or a romantic date, a soiree, spent with lovely friends?
Is it really phones and tablets where true life now just ends?
Yes, it's life but virtual – you're never quite, quite there,
And so, what's the point of flying if you're not truly in mid-air?!
The emotions of life's spirit, reason, poise, élan
Is being lost, diluted, compromised by loads of online spam!

We're using much more memory, but it's stored on the cloud,
So, losing our own ability to RAM and gigabytes allowed!
And SSD's, more megabytes, LANS, the internet
And IoT connections mostly unknown yet!
We ever-longer sit before a pixellated screen,
Yet a whole real world just sits out there, waiting to be seen!
Is this the sum of human life, the nerds that we've become
With all this knowledge,
And the world viewed on an ever bigger a bum?

HEALTH & SAFETY

In the 1950's we were quite happy,
With common sense held in sway.
Now it's all "equality, diversity",
Or whether one is gay.
And the so called "hate crimes" causes rancour,
Where there never was before,
Reinterpreted by the ne'er-do-wells and courts,
So, lawyers can earn more.
And meanwhile there is burglary and rape…
Assaults with fearful knives.
Which the police hold less important,
Than hate crimes in our lives.

And climbing trees, or playing games,
Are now seen as danger threats,
To be resisted by the HSE –
Which only proves how more lunatic it gets!
Cheese rolling, fireworks, old cobblestones
And sports are all at risk of closure,
In case a minor accident could dent
Someone's composure…
But what is life without fun or risk
And possibly painful bruises,
Which take away the point of life
In case diddums a finger loses?

OBESITY

When she was young she was beautiful, with a trim
    and lithe physique,
A girl who turned heads involuntary, for all
    liked to sneak a peek.
But as life went on she spent much time not moving,
    but just sitting,
And stopped the gym and walking for PC
    games, movies, TV – unremitting.
She let her sweetheart leave her,
    the best man she'd known or seen,
To spend life on social media, and watching
    downloads on a screen.
To add to this big burgers, cakes, pizzas, choccies
    fizz and chips
Consumed our harpie's waistline, legs,
    then torso, face and lips.
She soon resembled something like a balloon
    with stumpy thighs
But felt nothing wrong, for her peer group
    shared her same expanding size.
And even when she found the stairs
    they soon made her short of breath,
She ignored the pain – for no more calories
    and moving to her was living death.
So self-control was not an option, and with that,
    no inner peace,
For she died a blob in a double
    grave, because she'd just rather be obese.

FELINES

In my life I've had many friends – mainly girls I have to say,
Because I find them prettier, more convivial in their way.
(I think I cannot say that now in case someone thinks I'm "woke."
But at least I don't now chat up girls – at my age that's a joke!)
Yet oft I came across a girl who'd on meeting cast a thrill,
But only to be soon eclipsed by a sudden, feline chill.
Yes, dear friends, the cat was there to subjugate advances,
Despite the come-ons, knowing looks, and coy, delivered glances,
For the cat means 'home' is a constant love,
    which though only there for supper,
Imbues a continuity, a calm, that any man would scupper.
So, whatever was her beauty, intelligence, rapport,
From then the only direction was fast towards the door!

In later life I came to see the wisdom of my choice,
For husbands who married girls with cats just never have a voice.
And while the cat rules silently, cheery hubby gets the blame
For any misdemeanour, while the cat just sits there purring,
    winning every game!
So poor hubby's always wrong, forever second best,
'Til he cannot bear it anymore, and leaves the feathered nest,
Charged with infidelity, being stupid…yes, the man
    takes all the flak,
But she worries not for when he's gone-the cat will still come back!

(ANTI-) SOCIAL MEDIA

Before the world went truly mad some thirty odd years ago,
One had one's thoughts – and openly – quite proclaimed them so,
Without the scourge of being "correct" or tacitly adhering
To many others' views of groupthink uniformity of hearing.
Now if today a Twitter feed is felt beyond the pale,
A torrent of abuse is had – you'd be safer if in gaol!
Facebook, chat rooms, Instagram, What's App, WeChat, sext,
Everyone knows what you've just done and what you're doing next!
Yet it's all within a rigid norm that's intrusive, full of hate,
Because your soul's displayed online and so easy to appropriate.
But the trouble is it's all controlled by some business's dark forms,
To make you feel intimidated and so promote their radical norms.

And try to make you think like them without polemic, sense or thought.
So, you go spouting blindly all the issues they have wrought.
But you're unaware of this 'cos all our peer groups do the same,
And don't discuss the issues, for fear of being to blame,
For bringing friends into your circle with whom you don't agree
And that would mean being cast right out – a true calamity!
Yet with more discussion and dissent you could play a role
As a balanced, normal person, with opinions to cajole
Your single-issue friends with arguments profound –
Increasing your vocabulary and clueing up all round!
But most of all, don't post your thoughts
On Facebook, Chatrooms or Twitter,
For you may not have your friends again
As group reactions can be bitter!

STATELY HOMES

We used to go to beauty spots to see the lovely views,
Now "experiences" are all the rage, as if reliving past old news,
A theme park here, a costumed guide, some lions or funfairs, too,
Which never would have been there with the owners in situ.
Now they live so far away, to escape the modern cold,
Living in a bungalow, whilst the mansion makes their gold.
And gardens crafted by the greats, like "Capability Brown",
Are trampled upon by tourists from some depressing, sullen town,
As they joke about the finest art which aristos would please,
Then stampeding past the statues in a rush for "real" cream teas!
And so, the Duke and Duchess watch as their home's invaded daily
Pretending to be welcoming and waving oh, so gaily!
Just watching all the visitors as they pass in teeming hordes,
Looking at their furniture and these still surviving lords.
But the zoning of their lives as "themes" must surely make them bitter
Especially when the crowds have gone, leaving piles of modern litter.

LITTER

Why do people drop spent cans, their bottle, wrapping, bills,
When doing so's, so anti-social, and causes many ills?
Like hedgehogs trapped in six-pack holders, stuck for evermore,
Or dogs consuming plastic pots and choking on the floor.
Pond life fish and insects find their breeding all awry,
Just 'cos someone drops their litter as they casually pass by.
Or bottles spoiling beaches – with sands a sea of plastic,
Marine pollution's terrifying and needs solutions truly drastic.
Yet people go on tossing it from car and boat or train,
As if they hate the planet with particular disdain.

One tiny piece of litter, a whole view can destroy,
While people come to beauty spots, their glory to enjoy.
Then leave their litter when they go – but it won't evaporate.
So why regard our heritage with so much loathing hate?
It pollutes our farmland, streets and seas, lakes,
    and pristine streams,
And rushes into oceans where its poison now demeans
The creatures we rely on to keep our earth alive,
For without them we've no future, however hard we strive.

And so, it's time that every packet, bottle tin or can,
Had deposits put upon them so that items once began
As waste can be returned and used again, again, again,
And not defile environments with squalid visual pain.
If fines were used to stop this threat upon our lovely land,
Of a thousand pounds per item dropped,
    then the practice wouldn't stand.
And our national debt could be paid off,
    for there's so much trash around
That soon we would be fully free of litter on the ground.

All it takes is a little care, a thought for other folk,
Who altruistically pick it up, because litter is no joke,
So, drop it not, and pick it up, so don't be a lazy twit,
Or soon our planet will be dead-and you and I along with it.

PC

I hear now police want the odd tattoo,
To match their uniforms as the boys in blue,
Standing proud with colleagues throughout the force
So they can look written-on as those who recourse
To their protection in pursuit of the law –
But does it make them feel stronger? – I'm not so sure!
So why do they suddenly wish to begin,
To promote their desires on their virgin skin?
With the usual scratchings and slogans festooned
About their persons – are we all doomed?
I find the prospect so very arresting,
For what if his scratchings are against my protesting?
Of if an officer attends a crime to abate
Placing his arm of the law tattooed with "Hate"?

TATTOOS

What's the craze for these body designs, which have
    swept in so completely?
They're everywhere - even on parts we only
    normally show discreetly!
Every inch of flesh is covered: indelible slogans,
    signs and pictures,
Proclaiming tastes and views imprinted without
    any formal strictures.
But what's the point? They're painful, dear and
    can never be removed.
Embarrassing when today's opinions become
    eventually disapproved.
So why the urge for proclamations which
    to me seem so insane,
And make people look like hoardings or some
    current ad campaign!
Making beautiful people ugly, and ugly ones
    even worse,
Oh, please don't indulge yourselves in this
    indelible lifelong curse!
It's become an obsession, this permanent inking,
A way of avoiding some serious thinking.
Yet if it's character or topics you wish to seek,
Just try personality – or learn how to speak!
How weird this self – décor in multiple hues,
For once we shed birthmarks – now they're
    swapped for tattoos.

LOCKDOWN BOREDOM

Whether locked in or locked out, it seems that these days
We're spending more time in some sort of haze.
We're bored with the weather, the house and the news,
And have read every book and become barraged by views
On YouTube or radio, Netflix and more
But still cannot get out the damn front door!
(Except for a walk if not deluged with rain
And find one we've not done again and again)

A laugh would be nice if some friends I could see,
But it's just not allowed, so it's back to PC!
And talking of which, I'd so like a laugh,
Which would cheer me up greatly by more than a half!
But the comedy programmes just make me despair,
As they're all woke signallers proclaiming on air
Their political bias, opinions, and hates
Masquerading as humour but sorry, it grates!

I've tried new languages, cooking and booze,
And knitting nine jerseys in multiple hues.
Just trying to be human, with so little chance
Of seeing many others in this mad lockdown dance.
No pubs, no restaurants, just statistics, spikes, and curves,
It's all so unnecessary, and which no one deserves.
So, I'm really depressed at what I can't do
And so will try something novel, by using a different loo!

1842 – SOCIAL DISTANCING?

(Signing of the Treaty of Nanking 1842 aboard HMS Cornwallis with envoys from Queen Victoria and the Qing Emperors to end the first of The Opium Wars between Britain and China. Painting reproduced by kind permission of Mao Wen Biao and Yang Keshan. Displayed in the Sea Battle Museum, Guangdong, China. Image © The Ancestral Quest by F. L. Ying (aka F.G.Kwong)

PANDEMIC

The Pandemic's over, we've all been told
But on that point I'm not at all sold.
For the cost has been such with businesses broken,
There'll be nowhere to go to and the joy's just a token,
Of what went before, when economies soared,
And life's pleasures were many, across the board.
Now with restaurants closed, pubs, theatres, too,
We're now stuck and wondering what to do –
Except for shopping and browsing stuck online at home
And dreaming of pleasures we now do alone.
With tax rises, clampdowns, and restrictions galore,
We still won't be able to live like before!

Yet a tiny pinprick with a certified jab
Is now the main hope from a world leading lab,
Which is making much money to help their bet,
To predict the next crisis, we don't know of yet!
Yes, the truth is this plague's just the latest pandemic,
Because there will be more – what we're doing today
    is all endemic,
To the demise of our planet, our greed and pollution
    are all totemic
Of how we've overexploited our environment – it's
    all systemic
To the world we're destroying with too much plastic.
Overpopulation, resource waste, which is all
    far too drastic
For our fragile earth to continue –
    and so, we must be quick,
As it'll never be saved by just one little prick!

A CONCERT

I went to see a concert in a church built before the Baroque era
And so, to witness music from a remoter time, not nearer.
The optimism swelled as over a hundred people drawn from our goodly nation
Entered this sanctum of godly warmth in a spirit of intense anticipation.
Then the concert began, and we all felt flat as so were many a dear musician,
Confounding what we'd dared not think when buying our tickets for admission!

Oh, how those stones must've flinched in pain and muttered copious prayers
For their rendering was less gritty than this ensemble of earnest players!
Their instruments were just not attuned to the promise of sweet rendition,
And it mattered little whether they were playing from the first or last edition!
The people lying there in their tombs who listened there so ghostly
Must have wondered if these players were in tune – well, not mostly!
And all the bishops, clergy, wardens, reverends there anointed
Were probably turning in their graves; and at least, extremely disappointed.

To think that their instruments, so beautifully made of metal, ivory and wood,
Could allow themselves to be played by those who were earnest, if not good.
And music which should lift the souls of even the omnipresent dead
Were glad to be buried beneath the floor in the catafalques of lead.

It was all such a shame as the music planned was beautiful and charming,
Composed when recordings, then unknown, made comparisons less harming.
But by the end, a chill relief was present in all those who'd come to hear
Boccherini, Telemann, Mozart, Bach, or even Meyerbeer,
All played with compassion and depth in many a different key –
But their prevailing thought was one of relief – played in effort in capital E!

CHAPTER IV

© Ian Stuart

Amdram Actor. Lives in Yorkshire. Poet. Author.
Played in multiple productions including:

Cat's Cradle by Leslie Sands

Mixed Doubles by Alan Ayckbourn

Murder Weekend by Frank Williams

Beach Day by Alan Wade

The Elephant in the Room

Poems from the Edge

SCULPTING WITH WORDS

A block of stone and a blank sheet of paper
At opposite ends of an empty room.

A chisel and a pen – choose your tool,
Am I sculptor or wordsmith?

The pen is my chisel, the paper my stone:
Words and letters will work for me.

Like a sculptor, I start with a writer's block,
Perhaps no shape in mind, so chip away.

Bold or subtle strokes define and clarify,
Until shape becomes form, resonance emerges.

Finally, it stands alone, the story told,
Solid in its shape, refined in detail.

The readers walk round the finished work,
View it from every angle, prod at every flaw.

I hear the comments, but it is my work,
It is finished now, set in stone.

STORMFLOWER

Uprooted by a great storm
Rescued after the turbulence and turmoil.
Inspected anxiously with care
Concern tenderly lifted; replanted.

Slowly, hesitantly testing new ground
In a new part of the garden now.
Learning to grow again
In unexplored, unfamiliar earth.

Turning its face to the sunlight,
A survivor of nature's cycle
Supported by life's forces
Strengthening its roots.
Destruction turning to protective care
Mindful, storms may come at any time.

THE PATH

In the narrow country lane, a supermarket trolley stands
Its frame distorted – its wheels on unfamiliar ground.
The dog walks on, following the path,
His distractions are at nose level.

We pause, he to sniff the hedgerow, me to stare across the fields,
To the hills far away – defining the horizon
Thoughts always surfacing but then turning back inwards
A constant recycling of harsh reminders.

At the end of the lane there's a golf course boundary
I see people in their own world, in their moment
Individuals walking, their companion golf clubs.
We watch a while, the dog and I, then turn back.

I look forward to seeing the trolley again, a familiar landmark.
I know you supermarket trolley my friend,
We are the same you and I, pushed along the path,
Then abandoned, left standing alone.

You will stay there unless someone moves you along
I can choose to follow the path onwards
Hope for a signpost now unseen.
The dog trots on.

(Ecclesall © Writers' Anthology
of Poems and Prose)

PURPOSEFULLY POINTLESS MOTION

The path looks different this time; narrower and smaller.
The rain and sun doing their work,
Empowering the hedgerows and undergrowth.
Seasons moving – nothing has stayed the same.

At first, I see no trolley and I'm anxious for its fate.
Ah, it is still there, almost hidden in the tall grass
Steadily engulfing it,
It lies on its side like a patient.

Nature's course runs as true as ever
The outward sign of the world's slowly changing cycle.
People and trolleys caught in moments within time's continuum
Our lives slowly fading in the steady passing of the seasons.

Nature is always ahead of us
She was there first, does not depend on us.
We pretend to make a difference, to stabilise the planet's health,
Floundering in the middle of an ocean, hoping to change the tide.

But nature moves steadily, without cares,
While our memories of the past and fears for the future
Stop us living in the present,
The unique encumbrance of the human mind.

Striving for progress towards an unsure tomorrow
With ever new expressions to take us forwards.
But no matter how much we push the envelope,
It will always be … stationary.

COMPUTER BLUES

Staring at the screen, tapping at the mouse,
So much for 'just one click' away.
I'd rather be cleaning the house,
Than sitting here wasting the day.

I blog, I pod, you pod, we all pod:
New verbs for the gadgets class to spout.
But here am I, the useless sod
Whose will to live is running out.

My search engine's useless, run out of steam
Stuck in its tracks with no station in sight.
So much for the Internet, Berners-Lee's dream,
Though I suppose it's just me who can't get it right.

Now the screen is still, the timer frozen,
The connection cuts out without a care.
An hour wasted, with all that devotion
To a box with its callous software.

PLUS CA CHANGE…

"All change at Crewe" bawls the train tannoy's call.
I feel just the same though, no different at all.
Change isn't that simple; we prefer to exist
Without the upheaval – and so we resist.

Does change really matter, what effect does it spur?
What are the occasions when it really occurs?
Those times when it seemed everything changed,
And nothing could ever be quite the same again.

When the twin towers fell, did you feel the world change?
Our safe, secure world had been rearranged.
Or do you remember the incredulous shock,
That day in the sixties when Kennedy was shot?

And do you remember the day
When Elvis Presley passed away.
Do you remember whether you cried
Against change on the day that Diana died?

When idols have fallen, cut down in their prime,
The world they were part of seems to change for all time.
Then we pick ourselves up and regain our grip
Change trains when they break down, continue the trip.

And will I be remembered after I've gone?
Or you, or anyone, centuries on
For changing the life courses of those who survive
Somehow hoping to influence other folk's lives.

So, the world carries on, ever turning its face
To the sun and moon every day, and our race
Follows the cycle of birth, death and growth.
Plus ca change, plus c'est la meme chose.

SEASONS GREETINGS

Emerging flowers bend to fresh April showers,
Circling and swooping, gliding and soaring,
Birds on the wing celebrate spring
Joy in the moment and hope for the future

Then summer comes, its warmth from the sun
Bringing light and strength to the day
Blue sky, green grass, but we know it won't last
As time moves the wheel onward again

The daffodils fade, leaves biodegrade
As they start to brown and fall
The birdsong dampened as long nights beckon
Like shadows down a distant lane

Dark rain pelting landscapes melting
Into descending mists,
Sun long retreated light defeated
By clouds and veils of washed out grey

The winter will come, hear the beat of its drum
As it waits its due time,
To shorten the days and take life away,
The harshest, the coldest of seasons

GALAPAGOS

Even now, decades later,
The all powerful image is still there in the camera of my mind.
The lunar, otherworldliness landscape removed from time,
Found on the walk from the boat through the island -
Volcano formed all those millennia ago.

Just six of us and the guide, treading softly,
Carefully past the dozing seals blocking the path
No fear for them, they have no predators here.
Past Sally lightfoot crabs, bright red,
Scuttling into the scrub.

A glimpse of a land iguana, pale yellow,
Squatting in the distance.
Then the surprise just about the end of the walk,
Around a corner a jaw-dropping supernatural scene
As if time suddenly stopped.

The others turned back down the track,
But I lingered among the primeval spitting sea iguanas,
Their glistening scales damp from sea moisture,
As a lone turtle, in this moment of serenity,
Slowly swam into a rock pool.

This was their territory,
I just the privileged onlooker
Somehow transported,
Tardis-like into their surreal world,
Their timeless, pre-peopled land.
I had to go, catch up with the others,
And I walked away, but I'm still there.

ELEPHANT

He was there again today, his shadow cast into the room,
Grey and gentle.
Conversations, hubbub noise and chatter
Sometimes fading as if slowly aware of the uninvited guest.

The regaining momentum, a crescendo of sound
Bubbling and cheerful.
But the pensive, observing creature absorbs it all,
Silently sitting amid the outpourings.

You may notice him there from time to time,
Patient and caring.
He will visit without invitation.
You will have no choice, he's too big to move…and won't.

Accept the nature of the beast into your daily life,
Your strength within.
He sits outside you yet is your shadow.
Don't reject the elephant in the room.

(Ecclesall © Writers' Anthology of Poems and Prose)

THE TENT

You get used to routine, the norm's the norm,
Norm lives next door, to my own home
Retired neighbours doing the daily chores,
Commiserating on the weather, outside each other's door

Trips to the shops, the odd weekend away
From just one such I returned the other day
The evening drive, but as I neared
And turned the corner, there's something weird

You don't expect such an obstruction
To be right there, no introduction
Such a strange and odd intrusion
Or could it be just an illusion

Where did it come from, whence was it sent?
Right in the centre of my drive stood – a tent
It really gave me quite a scare
It looked as new but there's no one there

It shimmered so, that pale blue dome
That nylon shell where no one's home
I never found who owned that tent
Or why to me it had been sent

WRITER'S BLOCK … AGAIN

The horror of staring at an empty page,
just white space waiting for inspiration.

I scented the stream of consciousness waiting
to be released to paper, thoughts all over the shop.

Through the mist of subconscious thoughts
the lines, then the pages, filled with random madness.

Of my writings, knots untied so that the strings grew
into their own garden of everlasting mature words.

At last, in a drunken euphoria, I showed the results
to Rebecca, whose response was to shoo them away.

Consigning them to the shredder of rejected lines
and it was as if my sunshine had turned to rain.

The words that had stumbled out onto the page
consigned to meaninglessness for the rest of their days.

Feeling so blue, such humungous despair,
I threw the booklet at the budgerigar.

Throwing on my anorak and scarf I galloped off on my horse
with a blood tingling cry reaching far into the night sky.

I was gone, vowing never to return
to my creative writing course.

THE A to Z of CRIME

Anna advanced and, approaching Alison, asked anxiously, 'Are Adrian and Andrew alright?'
Both boys become braver beyond believe. But best be busy, better board bus. 'Bye Bye.'

Before coffee, Colin called concerning Carol's cousin's calamitous condition.
'Did Doctor Dawkins diagnose diabetes, darling?'
'Doctor Darwin definitely discounted diabetes.'
'Damn! Did distinguished Doctor Dawkins discard different dangerous diseases?'
'Defiantly!'

Endless examinations eluded enlightenment, eventually every eminent expert exhaustedly eliminated explanations.

Father Frederick fretted. Finding faith failing, forever feeling frustrated, Father Fred fearfully faxed forthright facts.

'Good God.'

He hurried homeward, having harrowingly heard how hopelessly her health had hindered her.

I interrupt in introducing increased intrigue into Isobel's in-laws' illness, intrinsically implying illegal involvement in its instigation.

'Jumping Jehovah!' Justin jeered jokingly. 'Just kindly keep keen, kids. Let's look logically. Many meaningful motives might manifest, money, malice, monstrously maybe…murder!'
'No! Never!'
'Namely notorious nurse Nigella's nephew's nefarious needs,' opined Ophelia.

'Obviously. One overdose of opiate on otherwise ordinary offerings of painkillers plainly produces predictably potent poison.

Quite quality quackery.'
'Quiet.'
Restlessly roaming round, Roger reflected, 'Remember, recovery requires really radical recuperative remedies. Someone should show sympathy. Strong steroids speed strength, so…

'Sh..t. Sodding sh..t!' Tragically, Tourettes tended to torment Tony.

'Temper, temper, try to talk tactfully, Tony. Think. Truth tablets traditionally tend to thwart tyrannous tormentors' transgressions.

'Tremendous!'

'Turning up unannounced undercover, using uniforms, unarguably unmasks ungodly Ursula's uncle's unacceptably underhand, unpardonable unlawfulness. Upshot?'
'Unpleasantness unveiled! Understand?'

' Utterly.'

'Unanimous?'

'Undeniably.'

Using utmost urgency, vigilant volunteers visited villainous Vincent's vestry, vowing vengeance. Violently vomiting, Vince verbosely voiced vital veracity, vividly venturing various vulnerable victims.

'Very valuable vicar. Viciously vindictive!'

When Wendy weakly woke, we weighed what we wanted, wondering whether we would watch wanton wrestlers writhing. We wavered.

'Well?' Will was waiting.

' Women wrestlers! X-rated?'

'Yes you zany zealot!'

'Zounds!!'

THE ELEPHANT IN THE ROOM

In the grand room, where the fine wines flow,
The conversation sparkles and the chandeliers glow
But when the chatter quietens, some sense he's still there,
Yet deliberately shun the temptation to stare

'I am what I am', the elephant says
'And I do what I do every day
I am what I am, and I sit in the room
And wait as I hear what they say'

The family gather in sorrow and grief
In the lounge where the talk of tomorrow is brief,
As they comfort the widow in her time of despair
For they all know that the elephant's there

'I am what I am' the elephant says,
'And I've seen the way that you pray
But I think that you know that it won't change a thing,
For I'll be back again every day'

The counsellor's group assembles each week,
They sit in a circle and take turns to speak
Of the hurdles they face and the trauma they share,
And they're all quite aware of the shape sitting there

'I am what I am' the elephant says,
'So I'm here among you today
But I didn't ask to be put in the middle,
And I resent being stared at this way'

And if you find you're alone in a room
At a time of upheaval, aloneness and gloom,
You cannot avoid him and will want him to go.
But he will just sit there and want you to know…

'I am what I am', the elephant says,
'And I go where I get in the way.
Though you wish I would leave, I will sit in your room,
For I'll always find somewhere to stay'.

CONGRATULATIONS!

I will make you a millionaire:
No need for a long questionnaire.
Your name's been selected,
The procedure perfected.
Once your details are found,
You'll be sent a million pounds!

Now I know you're in Sheffield,
But finding you is a minefield.
I could send you the cash by a truckload
For if you'll just give me your postcode,
But I can't be too sure
That'll it get to your door.

So, give me your bank account details,
Much safer than trusting the mail,
And things can only get better
As you'll soon be a real jetsetter.
Put aside any worry,
Just contact me now, but please hurry!

Well, hello there my generous friend:
Now I really don't want to offend
By declining your offer to fill up my coffers,
But I'm happy enough without yet more greenstuff.

I have all that I need,
So, I think you'll concede.
There are those more deserving
Of your kindness unswerving.
So, I won't go ahead:
Let me help you instead!

This may sound quite mysterious
So, to show you I'm serious.
I'll give you my house
And I'll throw in my spouse,
And send a token cash amount
To your bank account.

Your email was quite unexpected,
And I should be feeling dejected.
But I can see a new life,
Just me and your wife.
In the house where you live –
Yes, I feel quite impulsive.

I've had little luck to be frank
In finding people's banks.
I've been sent much abuse
And I feel there's no use
In my carrying on
With what's clearly a con.

I trust you do what you say,
So, send me your wife right away.
She can bring the house deeds,
That's all I will need.
Thanks. I'll sleep soundly tonight –
You have shown me the light.

THE CURIOUS CASE OF SANDUNES.

'Please stop rambling, Rose.'

Mr Robinson was very worried. Their beloved family cat, Stitches, had been missing for two days now and the children were distraught.

Just then, their faithful boxer dog known affectionately but inexplicably as Sandunes, bounded into the room, and jumped up excitedly at Mr Robinson's leg.

'No Sandy!' said Mr Robinson sternly, 'I've told you not to do that, you naughty dog!'

But their devoted hound seemed to be acting differently this time, as if trying to tell him something.

'I think he's trying to tell me something,' Mr Robinson said to his wife. Mrs Robinson looked intently at Sandunes, who was jerking his head repeatedly towards the patio door and cocking his rear right leg in the same direction.

'What's that, Sandy?' she murmured, gazing into the dog's eyes. 'Stitches has fallen down the old disused mineshaft at the bottom of the garden?... You clever dog!'

With that she and Mr Robinson dashed down the well-worn path, across the garden, following Sandunes, who suddenly veered off into the shrubbery and stood waiting over a newly dug patch of soil.

'What have you got there Sandy?' asked a puzzled Mr Robinson. 'Never mind that, let's go and find…'

His voice dropped as his eyes fell on the unmistakable sight of a black furry tail protruding from the ground. Sandunes looked up at the Robinsons. He licked his lips at the prospect of finishing off the tasty feline meal he had interned two days earlier.

The following week, Sandunes was reclining on the animal behaviourist's couch, where his disillusioned owners had sent him following the earlier unfortunate incident – to which, in his opinion, they had completely overreacted.

'You see doctor,' grumbled Sandunes, as he slurped down a second spoonful of chocolate. 'I showed them where their precious cat was, just as they wanted, and this is how they treat me!'

Doctor Saltwind, though, wasn't listening properly. His gaze was drawn to the large elephant sitting in the corner of the room, who had determinedly and immovably positioned himself there and was demanding their attention…

WHAT, ME GRUMPY?

'I've not been sleeping well,' growled Bronson.

'And how does that make you feel?' asked his counsellor.

'How does it make me feel?! Oh, just great!' Bronson snarled. 'How do you think I feel? I've had everything this week – cold callers banging the door and ringing me at all hours during the weekend, selfish people in restaurants with no consideration, talking and laughing at an ear-splitting volume, so you leave feeling more stressed than when you arrived, and with Richer-scale tinnitus thrown in.'

'I see. And how does that make you…?'

'Not to mention sodding cyclists, oblivious to everyone, riding two abreast when you want to get home quickly and slow drivers dawdling along or blocking the road with their eight-point turns into amply large parking spaces. Just confirms my theory – anyone driving slower than me is an idiot and anyone driving faster is a maniac.'

'Well, shall we pause to think…'

'And another thing,' Bronson was twitching in aggravation now. 'Horse riders on the road. Not only going half a mile an hour, also two abreast, but what about the mess the horses dump? Tons of it – no thought of clearing it up. If you had a dog, you'd be fined for that, and this is ten times the amount. How do they get away with it?'

'Erm, I see what you mean…'

'And it's no better on the pavement. I went to Sheffield on Wednesday. Don't get me started about the sodding bus service. Waited nearly an hour for one, and when it finally came, no apology or explanation. Anyway, as if cyclists, motorists, and horse riders aren't enough, you can't walk in a straight line without some mindless youth staring at his mobile phone barging into you. And when you do escape into the slightly less irritating environment of a "store" – used to be shops in my day, sodding Americans – you spend forever finding and then getting sense out of some gormless spotty teenager with the customer service attitude of minus zero. Yes, well. So how does it make me feel? Maybe it's this cold grey weather, maybe I'm just getting old – feeling generally under the weather. So, let's just say it makes me feel…'

He paused and then snorted sarcastically. 'Rather a bit grumpy then… Funnily enough, on reflection I now feel better for that.'

Gracing the counsellor with a vague smile, Bronson rose to leave.

THE CHEF'S SPECIAL

I'm just thinking back to a summer's day in Bakewell last year.

The little café I had wandered into at midday with Jack was surprisingly empty, a quiet relief from the bustle of locals and tourists outside. It was sparsely fitted out; a tiled floor, plain white walls, half a dozen wooden tables, none of which bore a menu.

On the wall, however, a chalked board advertised the fare on offer.

"Soup of the day £2.50
The Chef's special £8.99
Chocolate Surprise £1.80"

A sullen looking youth sporting various ear and nostril furniture approached with an order pad and a chewed biro.

'Yes?'

'Hello – hi. What's the soup of the day, please?'

'Same as yesterday – chicken.'

'You don't have a different soup of the day each day then?'

'Nah, it's yesterday's soup. The day was yesterday.'

Jack sneezed loudly, causing the youth to jump back in alarm.

I sighed. 'Right, so what's the chocolate surprise?'

'There's no chocolate, that's the surprise.' He looked at me contemptuously. 'Why do you think it's so cheap?'

My culinary options were rapidly being rapidly whittled down, but I gave one last try. 'And the chef's special?'

Suddenly, the lad's face lit up. He leaned towards me and conspiratorially whispered in my ear. 'He certainly is.'

'What?'

'Mind you, I'm biased. He's my dad, but his speciality is to die for!'

Now he had my attention. 'So, what is it exactly?'

'Well…do you like steak or beef?'

'Oh sure. Is that what it is, beef?'

He hesitated, thinking. 'This will taste better than the finest beef you've ever had! This particular dish is his passion. You won't be disappointed. I guarantee it.'

Well, I was hungry by now and I was hooked. I looked at Jack and decided. 'Ok. The chef's speciality it is.'

With a satisfied grin, the youth scurried off and disappeared through a door at the back.

As we waited, I idly watched the crowds drifting around outside and eagerly anticipated my meal. After about fifteen minutes, the alluring smell of roasting meat drifted in from the kitchen. We both sat up, sniffing the air, savouring the aroma. When it made its appearance, carried proudly in by the chef's son and set down with a flourish the dish did indeed prove to be truly mouth watering. The taste was glorious, the texture divine: if this was beef, then it was in a league of its own. The plate clean, I sat back, replete, and called for the bill.

'That really was delicious. You were quite right. Where do you source such wonderful tender meat?'

He smiled. 'Oh, it's local.'

Jack looked thoughtfully at me. He began to vigorously scratch his left ear. Then he decided to lick his testicles before, loudly and without warning, he broke wind. I decided it was time to leave. Bakewell, it seemed, had more culinary surprises than just its famed puddings.

That was about six months ago. I recall it now because the date coincides with that mentioned in an article in today's Derbyshire Times, when a young boy disappeared in the centre of Bakewell. A father and son have just been charged…

FOUR YEARS ON

February 29th 2020

The sky burned red over the hills in the new February morning. The usual 6.30 am routine awaited Charlie and Daisy – half an hour around the village, through the recreation ground, past the Co-op and back for a well-deserved breakfast – perhaps even for Charlie the treat of toast, bacon and eggs courtesy of the old frying pan in his kitchen cabinet.

Daisy, a middle-aged, wire-haired fox terrier, pricked her ears to the sound of a distant cockerel's crow, the only noise to break the silence of the pre-traffic calm in that hour. Charlie, mindful of sleeping neighbours, quietly closed the front door and off they set through the gate and along their familiar route. Even at that time they passed a couple of pained-looking joggers and one of two fellow dog walkers who gave them a friendly "Morning" and a nod.

The recreation ground was empty that morning, no other dogs in sight and a stillness hung in the air. The usual circuit round the perimeter of the "lower field," and then around the corner towards the children's play area.

However, before they reached the bend, with the view obscured by the trees, Charlie could make out the creaking of one of the swings. With no sign of even a slight breeze, it had to be a child and his or her parents making the most of the early hour on this serene day. Although at the same time, he thought that surely the fenced-off play area would be normally locked at that time.

They rounded the corner and sure enough, a distant figure could be seen rhythmically soaring up and down on the far swing in the playground. Although they were still a hundred yards or so away, Charlie could see it was a girl, perhaps 7 or 8 years old, dressed in a rather old-fashioned pale green coat. She was alone, no watchful parent or guardian with her and seemingly oblivious to either Charlie or Daisy.

Heading towards the path running alongside the playground to continue their route, Charlie sensed the child was caught up in her own world and thoughts, as though she was staring straight through them.

Daisy suddenly pulled back, ears flat, tail down, and Charlie stumbled as he twisted back to tug on the lead. He turned to face the swings again and was astonished to see the girl was gone. The playground was empty and the swing motionless. There was no sign at all that she had been there – as though he had imagined it.

The experience stayed with Charlie for the rest of the day, preying on his thoughts. He and Daisy had followed the same path every day for over three years and nothing out of the ordinary had ever happened before. How could a figure just disappear within seconds? For the next few days he approached that bend through the trees with trepidation, half-hoping the girl would be back, drifting up and down on the swing. She never was.

February 29th 2016

In the fading light of the late afternoon, Mary sat on the bench next to the path opposite the playground, alone with her thoughts. It was the anniversary of her daughter's disappearance, although the date only occurred every four years. There had never been any clue, any evidence to explain what happened that afternoon. Mary had made the fateful decision to post a letter. She had only left Charlotte for two minutes, but when she came back there was no sign of her. It was a decision that would haunt her forever. She would be back here at the same time every four years – every 29th February.

CHAPTER V

© Alexia Young and © Saskia Young

Twin Budding Artists and Writers aged nine.

"The Art of Words is like Music to the Ears"

*Dedicated to the passionate and inspirational teachers at Hampton Junior School
And to the joyful and enduring friendship of its pupils.*

An Eclectic Selection of Poems and Short Stories

Alexia Young

REFUGE

There's a tremendous disaster here.
We will have to flee and scatter.
They have bombs up their sleeves.
Leave all our things behind
Seeking for safety,
I see shelter.
We are safe.
It's a new place.
Hope.

There's a tremendous disaster here.
We are forced to run and hide.
They have bombs up their sleeves,
So, leave all our treasures behind.
Seeking our safety
We need refuge!
Let's hide out.
A new home.
Peace!

GIRL

Once upon a time, there lived
A girl who was so rude.
She broke into the neighbour's house
And ate up all their food.

She went into the next room
To find somewhere to sit.
She found a chair, but sat too hard
It broke into several bits.

She went upstairs to rest
And many beds she found.
She found the perfect bed to lie
That she went to sleep so sound.

Soon enough the owners came home,
They found the broken chair.
So, they went upstairs to check the bed
And found her asleep right there!

THE GIANT

At the stroke of midnight in the cobbled street, a hooded figure appeared. He was wearing a long, dark translucent cloak which made the wearer invisible. The hooded giant was carrying an old, shabby, brown-coloured leather case. Being silent as the night itself, the giant stalked the people in their houses. As he strode through the street, protruding at the bottom of his cloak were gnarled bony feet.

'Click!' The figure opened the case. As quiet as a mouse, the figure gently grabbed a jar full of magical dreams with a flick of his wrist. He conjured up a long trumpet-like horn to his mouth and blew. The luminescent liquid from it danced into the open window.

Curiously, a girl peeked through the window. She leant further to check that it was real. Simultaneously, the elongated cloaked figure quickly turned towards a reflection emerging from the shadows, his face shone in the light. The figure's face was crinkled and statue-like. The young girl gasped in shock. Extremely scared, she *quickly* wanted to close the curtain…

THE DREAMGIVER

In the dead of night, the Dreamgiver arrived at the orphanage carrying a sack of glowing eggs. He wore a bedraggled swamp-green toga and beetle-black spectacles. After checking he was at the correct address, he spread his intricate wings and floated as silent as the night itself into the orphanage which was filled with children. His gaunt body landed on the windowsill. Even though he looked like a monster, he was harmless.

The Dreamgiver placed the delicate sack of eggs onto a child's bed. Despite being careful, a boy stirred in his slumbers. The Dreamgiver felt alarmed, but the boy settled back into his slumbers. A wave of relief washed over him. One by one, he cracked the glowing eggs like when baking a cake. He was very quiet though. The golden eggs looked very shiny, bright and glimmering. 'Crack!' The Dreamgiver grabbed a golden egg. After opening the egg, the luminescent liquid spilled on to the duvets in the childrens' bedrooms. He delivered an astronaut that came from a book and a ballet dancer that came from a pair of elegant ballet shoes. The ballet dancer was dancing elegantly. The astronaut was floating in the air.

As the night wore on, he continued to deliver repeated dreams one by one to the children. He was busy as a bee. Suddenly, the boy stirred in his slumbers again. But then the Dreamgiver rushed to his bedside to find to his absolute horror, that an egg had fallen off the bed and on to the *Book of Nightmares!*...

ALEXIA'S DIARY – SAMSON

Dear Diary.

Where do I begin? Why would this tragic day come to me? Today has been the most devastating day I ever had. Father called me to the dinner table, and I knew something bad was going to happen to me. Mother was strange. She wasn't herself. She wouldn't dare look at me. Father had been acting oddly recently. I don't know why but I was expecting to be told off, but it was much worse. As I sat at the table, Mother and Father declared that I was going to school in England and that I was going to live with my Aunt Melanie and Uncle George whom I hardly knew.

I was more than heartbroken when Father said that he was going to sell my beloved dog, Samson. I was shattered. Father even said that my dog will be going to a breeder in France. Why would this happen? Why would my father do this to me? Father why are you betraying me at this moment? Please let me keep my pet dog. This is devastating; for me and for him. You have to know I really do love him with all my heart. He is truly my best friend, my sole companion, my guardian angel. How can you even think to do this to me.

If I am separated from him, my heart will break. You must not sell him to the French breeder. Just imagine, if he ends up behind bars, in a cage. To do this is too cruel. It seems as though you are disposing of us both without a second thought. I cannot bring myself to even look you in the eyes as I am so full of resentment. I shall carry the bitterness and pain of your betrayal with me forever.

Alexia

5th July 2023
Fern Electrics
5 Queens Bridge Road,
London W4 8XR

Dear Mr Fern,

Last Thursday I purchased a used electric scooter from your website. It was not until I got home that it stopped working and that it was in terrible condition. I also spent my own pocket money on this scooter, and it is a waste of money at a costly price for an electric scooter that does not even work.

In fact, one of the right wheels has fallen off while I write this. I feel very disappointed. If my expectations are not met, I will be forced to give you a damaging review and contact my lawyers.

I demand a full refund from your website and my money back. If this letter is not noticed in eleven days, this will escalate further, and I will contact the police. In my opinion, I hope for a new upgrade and a properly fixed scooter that can work.

Yours sincerely,

Alexia Young

Saskia Young

Monday 4th July

Dear Diary,

This morning when I woke up, I had a blazing hot temperature. I had a restless sleep; felt unsettled, nauseous. I felt numb. My whole body was numb. I shouted for my mother in desperate need. As I was drowning in sweat, my body was drenched from head to toe. My mother gave me an ice-cold blanket. She gave me ice cream. But unfortunately, my throat felt like lava when I tried to swallow. I was disturbed by the sound of chewing in my ear. As my throat was inflamed, my head was beating like a tornado. My muscles ached.

Tuesday 5th July

I felt terrible coughing throughout the night as my fever had risen. Today I woke up with my mother shouting, 'Stop coughing!' My mother was worried and so annoyed that she wanted to call the shaman, Nahtahlah straight away, because she was so fed up! I kept coughing throughout the night. So, she called him instantly. He was very concerned. He's never seen such a thing. They all rushed to my shelter.

When the shaman arrived, he asked me questions about my illness. The illness was mysterious. The shaman boiled up some rainwater over scorching flames. Then he put in some exotic crumbled-up flowers, leaves, berries, and some honey. The shaman stirred up the magical potion, then gave it to my mother. She fed me the medicine. I hoped to feel better tomorrow as my mother, and I had our fingers crossed.

Wednesday 6th July

It's a miracle when I woke up. I felt hyped up and got up today because I felt strong as a rock! I have no other words for it, so I said, *THE SHAMAN'S MEDICINE WORKED!*

I ran to my mother. She was speechless when I explained what happened. I really want to find the shaman to say thank you. First of all, I can sleep well. Secondly, I can now hang out with my friends Thirdly, I can now carry out my wish list of a load of ideas!

I walked to my friend's door, then hid, as I wanted it to be a surprise. Feeling well, then my friends and I swam in the pool of sapphire blue water nearby. After that we knocked on the shaman's door and gave the shaman a big hug. From that day onwards, I will remember where to go if my illness comes back.

MOUNT OLYMPUS

In the green fields just below the towering Mount Olympus lives a man. He is not just an ordinary man. In fact, he is beautiful as any god; incredibly tall and muscular. He has a handsome face and flowing curly hair like a young girl's. His eyes are as blue as sapphires as the ocean. And if anyone cast eyes on him, they are instantly jealous. You might call him a prince; but he doesn't act like one, as his personality is a weak as anything. He only cares about himself not others. Narcissistically, he spends most of his precious time looking at his handsome reflection in his golden mirror. When he opens his mouth, out comes a foul breath. When he talks, it is gibberish. It truly does hurt people seeing him. Anyhow, his heart is extremely sad and lonely as a solitary mouse completely abandoned and left in an empty nest.

THE SEARCH FOR ECHO'S VOICE

The yellow disc hung in the cloudless sky whilst the sapphire blue waters flowed gently past the blossoming flowers. Quietly weeping sat a girl with golden locks cascading down her back. Her skin is as smooth as silk and eyes as striking as emeralds. Her tears gently rushed down her rosy cheeks. Quietly she sat there weeping. Suddenly, a tall muscular man towered above the helpless girl. Enquiring, he asked the girl what was wrong. Puzzled by her mute response, he continued on his way. Frantically, the girl wrote a message and rushed after the man. After reading this note, the man with his handsome kind eyes preceded to help the fair maiden to find her voice, which had been lost. Instantly, they shared their names; the man -Theseus, and the girl – Echo, which she had written down. Then the man promised to help to restore Echo's voice.

'This special flower* (that could restore Echo's voice) could only be found underneath the lily pads growing in an underground swamp. 'We must begin this journey before the sun goes down!' exclaimed Theseus. 'Sundown. Sundown!' repeated Echo mouthing.

The journey was long, exacting, and painful for both of them. Just before the sky turned inky black, they arrived. Growing menacingly out of the underground swamp was an army of trees which were thorny and lethal in appearance. Feeling brave, Theseus put out his hand. 'Hold my hand. You will be safe!' Echo looked down. 'Safe. Safe!' she gasped.

Both took a deep breath as they entered the swamp. They knew that the legendary flower would be located underneath a lily pad. Suddenly a thunderous sound occurred. Both glared at one another. 'What could it be?' 'I recognise that sound, it belongs to the owner of the swamp, Cerberus' * warned, Theseus. Fear glazed over his face.

'Cerberus! Cerberus!' Theseus knew that he was in dangerous waters, but he remained calm and brave.

His initial thought was to swim in the swamp, carefully under the water. But then abruptly, a stem of a lily pad made a sharp snap. Suddenly Cerberus, scary and frightening with beady eyes and dagger-like teeth emerged from beneath the murky water and was coming *straight* towards them...

*(Legendary special flower from the swamp
– clash of colours of purple,
blue and green with a white centre)

*(Cerberus in Greek mythology
is referred to as the Hound of the Underworld
and is a monstrous multi-headed dog.)

SWEET MUSIC

My ears listen to music.
Under my feet,
I feel the beat.
Singing from the birds
I drift myself asleep.
So calm down now mum,
It's just music – sweet,
Music for my ears!

THE THINGY-ME-BLOB

I heard a noise creeping from beneath the bed.
Summoning up courage I bent down with my head.
A pair of glinting eyes kept staring at me.
The Thingy-me-blob grinning with a wicked glee.
It seems to live by hiding under the floor
Despite my throwing him out of the door.

It stares at me whilst I'm half-awake,
It grunts and it snorts whilst it swivels its neck.
'Get up you, lazy creature it seemed to say.
I pull back the blanket high over me instead.
Bury my face into the warm pillow it seems.
Hoping an actual end to a terrible dream.

All day and during the night he waits to dictate.
The Thingy-me-blob haunts the hours that I care.
The dream always ends in a horrific nightmare,
With that thing standing there at the end of the bed.
I shoo him away and scream out aloud,
But the Thingy-me-blob just stays there, leering a scowl.

The Thing grins laconically and jabs a finger in the air
To beckon me to follow him along the hall to downstairs.
Into the coal cellar, which he'd made it his home,
Hoping he stays there amongst the rubbish and gloam.
I slam the lock shut and push back the door,
But the Thingy-me-blob came back, for more, even more.

(*Young-Ying*)

FLYING TO INFINITY

You can really fly like her
in the fresh open air.
Amongst the scattered trees
and the scent of flowers of summer
if you really wanted to.
Just dare to dream a dream
with your eyes wide open.

For young and old
it doesn't matter, who you are,
Where you are, there are no limits.
because feeling weightlessness
You become one with the wind,
with the wings of nature.
Then throw off the shackles of gravity.

And so, reach for the sky,
without a care in the world.
Now take a chance
To fulfil those dreams and
you will soar higher and higher –
Flying effortlessly once again
naturally reborn like that little girl.
Having been released
from the safety of her mother's womb.
Try to believe in yourself,
to infinity and beyond.

(Young-Ying)

A CAT AT SEA

As the deep bright sun
sunk low on the horizon,
A lucky black cat went off to sea -
to seek his fortune
On a mountainous desert island,
however, nothing did he see:
But a vast expanse of water…
with nothing, but salty water,
As far as the eye could see:
for his paper-thin boat soon
Flooded with water,
and did he swim, or did he drown?
'Cos in real life how unlucky
A lucky black cat could really be.

(Young-Ying)

THE LIFE OF GABRIELA MISTRAL
(POET, DIPLOMAT, EDUCATOR)[1]

Introduction
Gabriela Mistral, an important South American in history was born on 7th April 1885 in Vicuna Chile. She died on 10th January 1957 at the age of sixty-eight. An inspiration to all, she taught herself to read at an early age and then went on to help others to learn.

Early Life
When she was young, Gabriela grew up with her mother and sister Emelina and brother Carlos in a small house in the picture-perfect Elqui valley, Chile.

Standing tall outside her bedroom window were the Andes mountains which she would often ponder about. Lying awake at night, she would imagine what wondrous secrets lay beyond the horizon and wished that she could explore them. As a child, she was a very inquisitive character and loved learning.

Ambitions and Dreams
Incredibly gifted, Gabriela taught herself to read so that she could tackle the most magical stories about princes, princesses, mothers and children, witches, monsters, birds and flowers. When she had time, Gabriela found joy in writing poems and loved telling stories – some happy and some sad, as well as singing songs. Being creative, when standing in front of her friends, Pedro, Sophia and Anna, she dreamt of becoming a teacher, teaching them the alphabet.

---

1 Born Lucila Godoy (father a poet) – pseudonym – Gabriela Mistral. In 1925 Appointed Chilean representative to the League of Nations and later to the United Nations Commission on the status of women.

Adulthood

Surprisingly at the age of fifteen, Gabriela's dreams came true as she became an elementary schoolteacher. She taught children of Chile who were then inspired to become teachers. During this time, she managed to publish over thirty collections of books and travelled around the world supporting children and improving schools. In 1945, her hard work was recognised as she became the first-ever Latin American writer to receive the Nobel Prize for Literature – an extremely prestigious award. Gabriela changed the lives of millions, teaching us to believes in the power of our voices. She was a dedicated, passionate visionary in her life, teaching us never to give up, whether we are rich, young or old, or where we came from! She helped to shape education, not only in Latin America, but also around the world. Gabriela will always be remembered for her outstanding contribution to education.

INDEX OF IMAGES

Tanya Ying ©
Etching: – "Four Figures" (Front Cover)
"Sunflowers" painting – acrylic (Front Cover). "Keep Fit Fiend" painting – acrylic.
Line Drawings: – "The Tree of Life". "The Fortune Teller". "Waiting for Him". "Cautionary Tale for Joyriders". "Nine Lives Well Lived" . "The Prodigal Cat". "Dreamgiver". "Alexia's Diary – Samson".
Photographs: – "A Day in the Country". "The Reluctant Knife". "Two Graces". "Balls of Cotton Wool". "The Old Oak Tree".
"The Butterfly Whisperers". "To Embrace the Seasons". "Faith, Hope and Joy Regained". "Christmas Present". "Seasons". "The Student".

Caroline Stuart ©
Line Drawings: – "If Only He Knew". "Girl in a Wheelchair". "A Spider's Web". "The Race, The Challenge, The Conquest". "The Greatest Itch of All".
"A Winter's Soul". "Cat". "The Path". "Elephant".
Photographs: – "The Vamp". "Poppy". "The Dormouse". "Felines".

Alexia Young ©
Paintings: – "The Magical Art of Words". "Floral Bouquet". "The Butterfly Whisperers". "A New Beginning 2 ". " A Cat at Sea 1".
Drawings: – "Temptress". "Refuge". "Girl". "The Giant". "Mount Olympus". "The Search for Echo's Voice". "Boodles the Flying Cat".

Saskia Young ©
Paintings: – "A Solitary Rose". "A New Beginning 1". "A Cat at Sea 2". "Sweet Music".
Drawings: – "Galapagos". "Thingy-me-Blob". "Flying to Infinity".

Edna Crone ©
Photo – Stone Rubbing – "Requiem".

W. Eric Ying ©
<u>Photograph:</u> – "The Girl in a Hat".

Barbara Jackman ©
<u>Photographs:</u> – "The Cultural Revolution". "Leaving the Ancestral Home".

Man Wen Biao ©
<u>Painting:</u> – Treaty of Nanking 1842. "Pandemic". "Social Distancing?"

(Reproduced by kind permission of artist/s)

ACKNOWLEDGEMENTS

Without the following people, this book would have never seen the light of day. First and foremost, I am indebted to my remarkable and forever-patient wife Caroline for her inspirational input and literary advice, as well as her imaginative line drawings. And, also to Edna Crone – being the first reader, for her constructive critique as well as to Anna Green for her striking design of the cover and her expert help in processing the manuscript to the publisher. I owe a massive debt to my amazing, creative daughter Tanya for her unique illustrations and photographic images, and not least, a huge thank you to her enterprising young daughters Alexia and Saskia for their special artistic contributions and unusual stories. At the same time, I take the opportunity to thank the dedicated teachers at Hampton Junior School who helped to inspire the latter with their vision and teaching. To my fellow writers, Simon Holder, Ian Stuart and the mysterious Juliet Smith, who I am still trying to trace to this day, my heartfelt thanks for their comradeship and collaboration. And to W. Eric Ying for teaching me to computerise and word process my work in the early beginnings in the first place. I must not forget the many exceptional individuals, who must remain anonymous for different reasons, who have inspired me on this journey with this illustrated anthology of verse and prose. And lastly, my unerring gratitude for the professional help and expertise from Carolina Santos, Andrea Johnson, Stephanie Carr, Jonathan White and Beth Archer from Troubador who went the extra mile to enable me to publish a worthwhile body of work.

EPILOGUE

A PERSONAL MESSAGE FROM THE AUTHOR'S PET MASCOT – BOODLES THE FLYING CAT

"Hope you enjoyed dipping into this book and found something that resonated with you to make your face smile and your heart sing!"

With oodles of greetings and thanks to wish every reader felicitous feline joy

BOODLES *the* Flying Cat.